CONSEQUENCES
(of defensive adultery)

M. Jane Colette

Also by M. Jane Colette

FICTION

Tell Me (2015)—an erotic romance for people who like a little bit of angst with their hot sex

Cherry Pie Cure (2017)—the award-winning "LOL rom-com for the sexting and blogging generation"

Text Me, Cupid (2018)-- a (slightly dirty) love story for 21st century adults

NON-FICTION

Rough Draft Confessions: not a guide to writing and selling erotica and romance but full of inside insight anyway (2017)—a non-fiction collection of essays about writing dirty, the power of words, taboo language, the freedoms and limitations of genre, fulfilling your creative drive, and the business of writing

SO TELL ME… where do I buy the damn books?

At all the usual book retailers, in print and e-format. For direct retailer links, visit **mjanecolette.com.**

Twitter + Instagram @mjanecolette
facebook.com/mjanecolette2
goodreads.com/mjanecolette
mjanecolette.com

CONSEQUENCES
(of defensive adultery)

an EROTIC
tragedy with a
HAPPY ending

M. Jane Colette

Cover Art: Michael C. Gray/Shutterstock
Cover Design: Sean Lindsay

GENRES were made to be BROKEN
121, 104-1240 Kensington Rd NW
Calgary, Alberta T2N3P7 Canada

First paperback edition

Library and Archives Canada Cataloguing in Publication

Colette, M. Jane, author
        Consequences (of defensive adultery) : an erotic tragedy with a happy
ending / M. Jane Colette.

Issued in print and electronic formats.
ISBN 978-0-9958102-2-8 (softcover).--ISBN 978-0-9958102-3-5 (ebook)

        I. Title.

PS8605.O4483C66 2017   C813'.6   C2017-901836-1
                                               C2017-901837-X

mjanecolette.com

for Sarah, Cheryl, and Nan

What's that?
—This? Nothing. A photograph.

He looks at the photograph, and demands a story I don't want to tell.

Isn't this what all women want? A lover who's passionately interested in the quotidian details of their boring, dysfunctional lives—as well as skilled with hands, and tongue, and cock?

No. Not me. Or do I? I start to talk. I tell him about… about all of them. And, inadvertently, me. Things I've never put into words for anyone before…

That's the game you and I are playing. Do you not know that? I am looking for the key. You're trying not to give it to me. But you want to play, and so you keep on talking, and so eventually, you will.

I'm careful not to say too much. I am not going to take my sociopathic lover of the moment into the tragedy of my life.

Why not? Tragedy is erotic. The things that make you laugh don't make you hard. Or wet, lover. Check yourself.

Fuck. Really? I'm doing this? Why?

Because you want to. Because you're compelled. Does it matter? Just talk.

So. I do.

CONTENTS

THE PHOTOGRAPH

WHAT'S THAT?
  —THIS?
Yeah. That.
  —Nothing. A photograph.
I'm not blind, lover-mine, I know it's a photograph. Of whom?
  —Everyone. Family. It's from Christmas.
Now there's a facet of you I did not know about. Nor suspected. Such sentimentality. Sweet.
  —My sister-in-law had them printed. Gave it to me the last time I saw her, I guess. I slipped it into the iPad cover. It must have fallen out when you were rummaging through my bag for condoms.
Ha. That's more like the Elizabeth I know and fuck. But the one in this photograph doesn't look like the Elizabeth I know at all. Jeezus. What's wrong with your face?
  —What? Nothing. I'm smiling. I'm just smiling.
Grimacing. Grinding teeth. Almost in physical pain. I've seen you smiling and in ecstasy and in pain, Liz, and—well, there's no pleasure in any part of you in this picture.
  —It was a hard night. You know. Christmas. Family. High tensions. Stresses.

Tell me about it. About them. Who are all these people? My God, did you cook for all of them? In an apron? Tell me you wore an apron.

—Talking about my dysfunctional family is not going to put me in the mood to fuck again.

It doesn't have to. That's my job. Come on. I'm curious. And, isn't this what all women want? A lover who's passionately interested in the quotidian details of their excruciatingly boring, dysfunctional lives—as well as skilled with hands, and tongue, and cock?

—Fuck you.

You have. And if you tell me the story to my satisfaction, you will again.

—You really want to hear this?

Absolutely. The tension is palpable—it jumps off the mildly fingerprinted surface. Just look at your face again. And the man next to you—is that your husband?

—That's Brian, yes.

He looks like he's restraining you, keeping you from running out of the frame. Terrified you will leave. The photograph or his life? I'm full of wonder.

—You're reading too much into a grip on an elbow.

Then correct me. And that? That's your daughter? What's her name?

—I prefer that you don't know her name.

Interesting. Understandable. But it will make telling the story cumbersome. Let's call her... Alexandra. She looks happy.

—She is. She was—it takes a lot to spoil a child's Christmas.

Next to her is?

—You insist on this?

I insist. Indulge me. Here, I'll reward you. You may keep one hand on my cock as you tell the story.

—Such a reward.

I'll put both of my hands between your legs. Stroke you when you please me.

—Pervert.

Name-calling does not please me. Who's next to... what did we call her? Alexandra. Who's next to Alexandra?

—That is Brian's ex-wife. Zia.

Gorgeous. Egyptian? And may I say, lover, your lack of jealousy pleases me. I reward you, a little.

—Ah, fuck.

Talk.

—She's as Egyptian or Arab as I am French. Canadian, in other words. Born here. As for lack of jealousy... well, it wasn't my idea to have her there, for Christmas. It was the first time that's happened in 15 years. But you're pushing ahead of the story.

Indeed. I'm impatient. You know that. Still. We should do this properly. Continue with the cast of characters. Kneeling at her feet? Love that pose, of course.

—That's Stefan. He... well, that's hard to explain. In that moment, in that photograph, he'd be Zia's... boyfriend.

Such a juvenile word when used in relation to a man fucking a 50-year-old woman. Lover?

—Well... that depends on what you understand by the word.

I can't wait for you to explain that part of the story. The wife, the husband. The daughter. The ex-wife. Her—ha!— boy toy boyfriend. This angry young woman—the only person in the picture in more pain than you, lover—this must be the daughter of the first marriage?

—Yes. That's Brian and Zia's daughter.

Her name?

They called her Destiny. But she... she changes her name, later. When Alexandra is born. To Sasha.

Destiny-Sasha. And I get to know her real name? Mmm. Fascinating. I'm allowed to know the stepdaughter's real name. Does she hurl accusations of favouritism and evil stepmotherness at you?

—All the time.

As she should. Now, this woman? She's the reason I'm forcing you to tell the story, you know. As soon as I looked at the picture, she jumped out as its centre, focus. And yet, there she is, at its edge. Almost out of frame.

—I have to stop fucking artists with high EQ. Yes. That's what she is. The centre. The focus. That's Annie. My sister-in-law. Brian's brother's wife. She's the reason—she was the glue that made us a family. And the catalyst... Fuck, I don't know how to explain it. She's the reason—the reason everything unfolded as it did, I think.

Catalyst? Everything? This gets better and better. And you wonder why I want to hear the story. But wait. There's Brian's brother's wife. And where, I must ask, is Brian's brother?

—Oh... you're right, he's not there. He was there, I'm sure he was there. He must be taking the picture.

Brian's forgettable brother. Does he have a name? Wait— don't tell me. Not yet. I like him nameless, behind the camera, in the shadows. So. That's the cast. Now put the picture over there, in that bowl of walnuts... and now, both hands on my cock. And tell me everything. I won't distract you too much. Except when you get to the really good parts.

—I have no idea where to begin.

At the beginning, of course. At the photograph.

—That's not the beginning. That's practically the end.

Well. Then begin with the thing that's most important to me. When you met me. It must have been around that time. I recognize the haircut. And those shoes.

—We met a few weeks later, yes. But you're not part of the story. Not at all.

You're so wrong. Every story before you met me is the backstory to… well, why you're here. In my hotel room. Naked. Beside me. Beneath me. With me. So it's, really, all about me.

—Narcissist.

I prefer sociopath. Still. I'll indulge you. Never mind me. Start with her.

—Her? Annie?

Yes. She is the catalyst, you said? Anyway. She is where you should begin. I want to know her intimately.

—I don't. I didn't.

But you do, don't you? So. Talk. But keep in mind… I'm easily bored. And I only really like one type of story.

—Am I telling a story to you or to your cock?

We are fully integrated. One and the same. And what a perfect feedback loop you have. Now. Impatient. Begin. Tell me about you and Annie.

—Then I have to tell you about me and Brian. Brian and Zia. Zia and Annie… All of them, all of us.

Hmmm. All right. Go ahead. But start the story with something hot.

—How about another photograph, a thoroughly inappropriate one, texted to the wrong number?

I love it. Go.

PINK PANTIES

IT HAPPENS WHEN I'm packing up to go home—wondering when the paperless phenomenon will hit corporate litigation, wondering whether I should bother bringing this shit home anyway, because it's not that important and what I want to do—what I *will* do when I get home—is watch *Sherlock* with Alexandra. Unless Brian is home, in which case the papers will be a reason to not spend time with him after Alexandra's bedtime.

Holy fuck.

I can't believe I just thought that.

My phone pings. The random, unassigned ping of text messages from random people. Brian has a special sound—and also instructions to only text me if it pertains to Alexandra. Alexandra has her own sound, of course—I am distracted, briefly, by the thought that my ten-year-old has a cell phone, the world we live in, fuck. Sometimes, my lover of the moment has his own ring.

Do I?
—Yes.
Good. Come here, on my lap. Love that phrase, by the way. Lover of the moment. Although it also, strangely, demeans me. A fascinating feeling...

Ping.

Sometimes I love the promise of the random ring. Who is it? What news? What consequences? If I have just exchanged telephone numbers with someone new... is it him? Where will it lead? My heart beats faster; I am excited.

Sometimes, I resent it as a horrible distraction—I stare at the telephone with hatred, I want to pretend I did not hear the sound, I wish I'd had the foresight to turn off the ringer.

In that particular moment, I am neutrality incarnate.

And then I'm not: it's Annie, and I know what is coming. A plea, a request, a twisting of my arm. A threat. A dose of guilt. Sometimes I sidestep it, avoid it—with rudeness, curtness. Or don't respond at all. Sometimes, I fall into it, and wonder how the fuck she manages to make me...

How does she make you?
—If you keep on interrupting me, I will never get to the dirty picture.
Ha. My imagination is working overtime. But if you continue at this torturous pace, I will engage in a torture of my own...
—Aaah...
Talk...

Ping. Annie.

An image.

What the fuck.

It's a photo of delicate, tiny, lace panties. Pink. So see-through, there is darkness of an unshaven mound of Venus. Also visible is the first curve of a white thigh, a swell of belly, the shadow of a belly button.

I love that phrase. Mound of Venus. Who says medicine must be clinical?

What the fuck?

I hold the phone in my hand and look at the pink panties, perplexed. From Annie.

OK. Clearly, not meant for me.

There are places my mind does not go: I imagine Annie as neither the wearer nor the sender; Brian's brother as recipient seems ludicrous. The existence of this photograph and its appearance on my phone make no sense. I can't process.

I ponder what the right etiquette here is. A "missent text" text to Annie?

Or pretending I didn't get it?

I decide—I do this with almost all apparently difficult, yet ultimately unimportant decisions—to do nothing.

I'm putting the phone away, when it pings again.

"I'm so sorry, Elizabeth. Please delete. And tell me you did so, OK?"

Of course, I delete. But I don't respond. Ugh. Acknowledging the existence of the photograph just seems... distasteful.

Do you never send pictures of yourself in panties—or without—to your, how did you put it, my glorious slut, lover of the moment?
—Never. I am a ruthlessly ambitious lawyer, with perhaps political, and definitely judicial, ambitions. And we live in a most hypocritical age.
I think I will start demanding skanky photos of you just to have blackmail material handy for when you start your political career.
—What makes you think I will comply?
This.
—Ah.
Yes?

—Mmmmm. More.

Greedy. The price is a skanky photo of yourself—preferably without pink panties—when you get home. Now. Continue.

I pay for my lack of response—my false delicacy, I suppose—when I pull up to the front of my house, and Annie is there, waiting for me on the porch.

In a state.

I see her, waiting, pacing, as I park. And I want to hide in my car. All I had to do was text, "Done." Fuck.

And now. What? Explanations I don't need or want to hear.

"Elizabeth," she says as soon as she sees me getting out of the car.

"I deleted it," I say. "Of course."

"Thank you," she says. "And… please… if you could…" she is blushing and stammering, and she is younger than Sasha.

"Of course I will not mention anything to anyone," I say. Awkward, stiff. Unsympathetic.

"Promise?" she says.

"Christ," I snap. "Pinky swear, cross my eye, and hope to die?" I walk past her and to the front door. Unlock it and walk in. Do not invite her in. Close the door behind me.

I pretend I don't hear the gasp and the sob. I wound her. I shut her out. I do this on purpose, because I do not want…

Ours is a relationship of convenience, and not of confidence, and I want to keep it that way. I don't want her close. I don't want to know—who, why, what.

Your sister-in-law is fucking around, and you turn into a prude.

9

—No! Nothing like that. I just... don't want to know. That's how it has been, between us, since the beginning. I don't want to know...

And do you find out?

—Yes. But it takes a while. I don't want to know her. I don't want her in my life, I don't want anything to do with her...

But?

—She's persistent.

HARD TO OPEN

ANNIE'S PERSISTENCE IS the reason I find myself… in places like the meeting room of the Louise Riley Library, sitting at a table with the sister-in-law I don't like, the ex-wife I hate, and the stepdaughter who hates me, and several random strangers I do not want to know… being assigned a grade school exercise.

"Write down four things that are hard to open," Annie instructs. She's the facilitator. Of course. I chew on the cheap yellow half-pencil she provides. The question has something to do with a book I don't own, haven't read.

Stop. Stop right now. I do not want a fucking chick lit book club story. Unless you're reading porn.
—We're not reading porn. It's one of those god-awful self-improving Oprah books.
Look at me. Flaccid, immediately. Fix this.
—It's quick. I last one session. And it will show you, better than the photograph, why… it will show Annie. And me. And fucking Zia.
You in a room with the ex-wife you hate makes my cock twitch a little. Go. But quickly. And don't you dare tell me anything about the book.
—I won't. I never bought it: I don't even remember the fucking title.

11

But there you are.

There I am. And there, just as out of her element and just as unwilling, is Zia. How the fuck does Annie do this? Put the three of us—Zia, Annie, and me—up against a wall, in an identity parade, and Zia and I both will come across as powerful personalities. Annie?

Soft, so soft. Liquid.

But the soft excel at manipulation.

How does she get me here? Always, like this: "For Sasha," she says. "Sasha needs this." Does she, really? I never know what Sasha needs. But all I ever hear from her is that Annie, her beloved godmother, is the only person who understands her.

So, I comply...

To Zia, she must say something else. Not "Sasha needs this," although you'd think the doting mother would be more likely to be worked on by *that* than the unwilling stepmother. No, "Sasha needs this" will not work on Zia, because Zia knows best what Sasha needs and will not accept input. To Zia, she would say... What? "Elizabeth said you *wouldn't* do it." That might work. Even Brian uses that one. "Elizabeth didn't think we should even raise this with you—she said you wouldn't even consider it," is a frequent, favourite opener of his. How she loves to prove me wrong—especially when I'm right.

And to Sasha? How does she sell the futility, *stupidity* of this exercise to Sasha? "Spend one evening a week with your mother, stepmother, and me discussing books you'd never choose to read yourself!" Seriously? What teenager would ever, ever do that? Perhaps a compliant, attached, family-focused one—perhaps there are such beasts—but pierced, tattooed, rebellious "how can I get a rise out of my parents today?" Sasha is not one of them. Yet, there she is. Sitting as far away from me as possible. Not looking at her mother. But, there. Present.

"For me," Annie would say to her, perhaps. That's all it might take. "For me." Because Sasha loves her, and that makes her vulnerable.

Easy to manipulate.

The soft are relentless, ruthless.

Soft, relentless, ruthless. Successful.

Mmmm. Like my cock—except for the soft part. Relentless. Getting ready to be ruthless.
—How is this getting you hard?
I think it's the vicarious experience of you outside your comfort zone. Fucking hot. Continue.

"Four things that are hard to open," Annie repeats.

Sasha groans. "Annie!" she remonstrates. "Really?"

"Please," Annie says. "Make a list of things that are hard to open. From the book. It's supposed to be… it's a central metaphor of the book. It's a great way of really getting to know…" Her voice trails off. Her eyes plead. Sasha starts writing. So do the assorted random strangers.

I bet Annie, facilitator, writer, coach, connector, communicator, self-declared empath, already knows all their names, and the names of their dogs. I don't recognize— see—their faces.

Zia is scribbling, doodling. I am certain she hasn't read the book, either. Like me, she probably hasn't bought it. We are terrifyingly alike, I know. My dislike of her is more than guilt over displacing her.

It is terror of myself, of what I could become. The mirror of all my ugliest, nastiest parts.

She feels me watching her. Scowls at me. Hates me.

I fight the urge to stick my tongue out at her.

Things that are hard to open.

Why am I here?

Why did I agree to this? I like none of these women, know as little about them as it is possible to know about people forced into your life because they are the baggage of the people you *choose* to have in your life.

That's right, Sasha, your evil stepmother just called you baggage.

What are you going to pierce to avenge yourself on me for that?

Does Sasha know her evil stepmother has a clitoral hood piercing?
—No. Strangely, it's never come up in any of our very few conversations.
You're a thing that's hard to open.
—I am. And so is each of them.

And so, when Annie glances over at my sheet of paper, she sees:

"Elizabeth.

Sasha.

Annie.

Zia."

Her mouth forms an "Oh." Then shapes into an upside down "U." I crumple up the paper. Get up and leave without a word.

I never find out if Sasha and Zia persevere with the book club. Perhaps they do. Annie, certainly, does, even if all of us abandon her. Even if it is only she and one other person at the rest of the meetings—and the other participant hasn't read the book.

Annie perseveres.

I don't hate her, you know, even though she thinks I do. I just… Zia is in my life, because she was Brian's wife, and, well, fuck, there she is. They made a child, and Sasha connects Brian to her, and through him, both of them to me. I must suffer them. Endure them. It is my responsibility to do so. I can't make them disappear—although, Christ, I so often want to.

Annie? She is married to Brian's brother. Whom Brian rarely sees, and would be quite happy to see even less often. The bond between them is thin. Tenuous. Were it not for Annie, perhaps it would have atrophied completely by now. But Annie preserves it. And she keeps on trying to create one between us—bind me to her. Somehow.

And it astounds me. Why? Why does she try? Because, if we just met as strangers at a party, bumped into each other in a coffee shop, were trapped together for six hours in a dark elevator—even went through the rigors of law school or grad school or articles together… we would not choose to be friends.

It is not just that I would never choose her. The incompatibility is mutual. She would never choose me.

We have nothing in common, she and I. Nothing. I'm a lawyer, she's a writer-artist-dabbler—which to me means flaky, under-employed. The mustard and jam jars we drink out of on our rare visits to her house appall me; her chipped Value Village china offends my aesthetic. Worse, it sends me back to a childhood I despise. And while she's never made a comment about the quality of my crystal or the price tags of my clothes… well. There is as much judgement in her eyes when she looks at my Armani suit as there is in mine when my eyes slide off her latest vintage "find." There is between us nothing on which to build a bridge—except that we are women married to two men born to the same and then fucked up by the same woman… but even that is not a bond because we never talk about them. So what is there to bind us?

Nothing.

But she chases me.

Reaches out.

Still.

Despite all the rebuffs.

She wants you to love her.

—An observation worthy of Oprah. Or Annie in her role as book club facilitator.

I know women. And I know that kind of woman. And I know the allure of the kind of woman you are. It's that you won't love. For the kind of woman Annie is your aloofness is as attractive as the aloofness, unavailability of an otherwise perfect lover.

—What the fuck?

Never mind. I already understand you and your sister-in-law better than you understand her or yourself. But maybe that changes a little through the story? Yes?

—Maybe. But before I get to any of that, I think you need to meet my husband.

Mmmm, yes. Let's move me out of my comfort zone. I like that.

ENTER THE ADULTERER

I AM A cliché: a twenty-something grad student who lets herself get seduced by her professor. Or seduces him. I'm still, 15 years later, not clear on the issue of agency. At the time, I suspect I like the story that he seduced me, that he chased me. Later, I prefer the version in which I was the active agent… and later still, I try very hard to absolve myself of any volition. It all happens to me—I don't *cause* any of it.

Except, of course—I cause it all.

It happens like this: I'm wandering down an over-crowded hallway at the University of Calgary's Professional Faculties Building, wondering whether a Master's degree is really worth anything and pondering tax implications of spousal support and child support and who the fuck cares, I don't—yes, in retrospect, that becomes hugely ironic—when I hear shouting. No, not shouting, projecting. Grandstanding. Voices raised and pitched; dropping. An argument? There is a clump of students. An explosion of applause. More words: two voices, like swords duelling. I am a lawyer—I am a litigator—*because* that kind of battle is my primary turn-on. I listen—and before I grasp the content of the argument, I identify the winner. And it's in his voice—the confidence, the delivery, the lilt. He charms me, seduces me, as he does the entire audience.

His opponent—who may, for all I know, have law and truth and right and justice on her side—is being charmed into submission too. Her arguments thrust aside—so very gently. Disarmed—almost lovingly. I suppose I fall right there, right in that moment, without ever seeing him.

And—the final thrust. I gasp, and so does everyone else. Applause. Thunderous. A whistle.

"Please, please, ladies and gentlemen, enough," the voice, pitched lower. "Now—as you were. Back to class. My friend," I don't see, but I imagine, an arm loped over the shoulders of the defeated colleague, "a pleasure crossing swords with you. As always."

"I wish I could say the same," the loser's voice. Tinged with bitterness, trying to be gracious.

"You were brilliant," he says.

"I was right," she counters. "You were…" her voice trails off. He was… what?

Fucking incredible.

Yes. That's when I fall. I want him.

The crowd thins out. And I see him. And he's…. really, nothing spectacular. He's not speaking. He's not looking at me—he's looking after the fellow professor he's just trounced, his expression… smug. I realize I know him. I've seen him around. He teaches constitutional law, criminal law. Wears his hair too long. The colours of his shirts are pretentious in their self-conscious refusal of the ordinary.

I need him to talk again. Desperately.

I need to impress him. I need him to be impressed by me. I. Need. Him.

"Elizabeth," I say, extending a hand. And now, his eyes are on me, and I am about to hear his voice again.

"Brian," he says, takes my hand. It's the voice, not the touch, that makes the blood in my head—other places—pound.

This is the moment that makes or breaks my life—I'm sure of it. This is the moment where I win or lose him.

"Teach me," I say. "I need to know how to do that."

And he laughs.

Still holding my hand.

"I would so very much love to teach," he says. "Anything you… need to know."

My Elizabeth finds her first alpha.

—I suppose that's one way of looking at it.

Does he fuck you that day?

—No. Three days later. In his office. I am entranced… I am so fucking easy.

You are young. Inexperienced. He gets off on that. And so do you. I bet you play up your inexperience. You like playing the role of the student. Yes?

—For a while. Yes. It is… exhilarating.

I love everything about it. I love the rapidity. The sordidity. The casualness and completeness of that first seduction. That first day, all he tells me is what classes he's teaching, and that I should sit in on one. God-awful, pointless undergrad courses I hated the first time around. But I want to hear him. Fuck, that voice—I need it as I've never needed anything before. And so, I go to one class the next day. And another. I sit at the back. Listen.

Your hand between your legs.

—Uh—no.

Yes. Now. Do it.

—Ah….

I don't think he sees me the first time, and I don't linger after. I'm embarrassed and I don't know how… what. The second time he sees me mid-way through the lecture and smiles—just for me. I fucking walk on air. As I get up to leave, he beckons me over.

"Crazy day today," he says. "But tomorrow, I have office hours, two to four. It's a slow time of year—I don't expect I'll have too many students. Come see me."

I'm there at 2:05.

"You're late," he says.

I'm wet.

"Do I look that eager?" I ask. Throat tight.

"So very," he says. He gets up from his desk and crosses to close and lock his door as I walk across its threshold. It's about three minutes later that I'm pressed against that door, jeans around my knees, his hand in my cunt. Ten minutes later, I'm on my knees, his cock drawing circles on my cheeks.

Fuck, yes. I'm revising my opinion of Brian. Respect.

Thirty minutes later, his lips brush my cheek, then my lips, for the first time. And he gives me a short lecture on the lost art of elocution while caressing my breasts. And then, nipping my earlobe: "And while I'm in no way complaining, next week, we're also going to work on your cock-sucking. Because you clearly need more practice."

His fingers move from my breasts to inside me as he says that and I groan, any sting to my ego subsumed by another orgasm.

For the next few weeks, I am completely, totally subsumed within him. Nothing else exists, nothing else matters. I sleepwalk through course work and lectures. My research is on autopilot. The two days a week I put in at my law firm to maintain my pecking order and keep my face in front of the crotchety old men who control my future financial destiny, during which I cannot see him, are torture. My weekends are spent pining. Fantasizing. I sit in on all his lectures. And I spend much of his non-class time in his office, sitting in his lap. Naked.

I'm not sure at which point I realize he has a wife and child. In the middle version of this story—in which I am not to blame for anything—this is knowledge I don't have at the beginning. I am not complicit in adultery. I am not enabling cheating. I am not a skanky slut—I am a woman madly in love.

Or lust.
—Definitely in lust.

It's not that he doesn't tell me. He assumes I know. Christ, how can I not? There is—the wedding ring on his finger. The photo of a beautiful woman on his desk. It clatters to the floor a couple of times when he takes me on his desk; once, I'm the one who picks it up, replaces it. Half-a-dozen if not more photographs of a girl-child, and childish art taped to the back of his office door.

I find out when, still in my fog of lust, I ask him to go to something with me. What is it? Maybe something at my law firm? Or maybe it's just dinner…

"Elizabeth," he says. "My love. My loveliest Liz. You know that's out of the question."

The voice, still beautiful. A touch, in that moment, patronizing, and I'm hurt.

"Why?"

And as he says, "Because I'm married," I hear, "Because I'm married, you stupid child, what the fuck is wrong with you?" and I burst into tears.

And he loves and consoles me. That is part of his charm too—part of the elocution-rhetoric-argument-logic lessons I get from him after we fuck, after I take his cock in my mouth. "Here are some other fabulous things to do with your mouth," he starts the lectures. And there are tips and tricks. But mostly: kill them with love. Disarm them with kindness. Love them and empathize with them as you're fucking them over—then their defenses don't come up until it's too late.

I don't remonstrate or protest. Of course, I should have known. Of course, he didn't try to deceive me. Of course, it's all right.

Except that it's not.

Is the youthful you torn apart by a moral dilemma?
—No. I wish she had been. But no. She doesn't even... none of it feels real. I mean, the wife, the child, that marriage. There's just Brian—and there's another life that he has that's separate from me. And that's OK. It doesn't matter. Nothing matters, but that voice in my ears—those fingers in my cunt—those lips on my earlobes...
Mmmm. I will follow those instructions for a few minutes... and now... catch your breath and... continue...

He makes the deceit and the sordidity—the need to meet *here* and not there, the need to not touch when we are in public, the need to give me the cold shoulder in the faculty lounge—he makes it all sexy. He makes me love it. When we are alone, he tells me what he was thinking of doing to me when he saw me pass by with my thesis supervisor. And then he does it. And I am completely enamoured. It is all I want, it is all I need—it is enough.

Until it isn't, and you want the wife out of the picture—and her picture out of his office.
—Well... no. That's not how this story goes.

THE WOMAN IN RED

I SUPPOSE ZIA enters my life the moment I start fucking her husband, but she becomes real to me the first time I *see* her. She is wearing a red cocktail dress that I immediately, in the inevitable arrogance of youth, think is too young for her. Also, red patent leather platforms and bright red lipstick.

Cock-sucking lipstick? The kind I want you to wear when you meet me, and you won't, unless I bring it to the hotel room?
—Precisely.
I like to get the visuals right. Speaking of which... let's put some of that on you for this part of the story, shall we?

It's unplanned, of course—by me, anyway—and I'm caught off-guard. Or am I? It's the School of Law's Christmas-do, and I'm only there because I think Brian's going to be there, and it's the weekend, and I never get to see him on weekends, and I. Need. To. See. Him.

Does he expect me? He must, at the very least, suspect I might be there. But we don't discuss the possibility at all beforehand. Still, when he sees me, he's utterly unfazed.

It doesn't occur to me then—not for years—that surely, he's experienced that kind of awkwardness before. He takes it in stride.

The introduction: "Zia, meet Elizabeth, one of our grad students. Elizabeth, my wife, Zia."

A polite smile, nod. A tepid handshake. Piercing eyes that take me in, evaluate me—dismiss me, or so it seems—and turn to the woman beside her. It's Annie—but I don't know that yet. I don't, actually, remember that she is there—she tells me, later, that's when, how we first meet. Claims Brian introduces us. I don't remember.

I think only of Brian.

Think nothing of his wife. Don't notice anyone else…

When we see each other a few days later, neither one of us alludes to the encounter—although it is that day, as he tongues his way down my torso, to my thighs, in-between-them and back up again—that I do have the thought: he fucks *another* woman all the time.

When he smears my wetness all over my mouth with his, I have this one: that woman is his wife.

And, finally, as he returns back to devouring my cunt, and I come, explosively: I am The Other Woman.

I am young, and naïve, and stupid, and in that moment… I think it's sexy. Hot.

So grown-up.

I am having an affair. I am an adult.

I am The Other Woman.

I love that that *turns you on.*
—That's because you have no morals.
I have a few. But I find "Thou shalt not covet thy neighbour's wife" the most satisfying commandment to break.

The second time I see Zia, she is wearing red pants, red stilettos, and a red pillbox hat. A red scarf peeks out from the top of her black jacket.

"Does she always wear red?" I whisper to Brian. We are hiding in the archway of a building. Zia appears in the street in front of us, as we are walking, arms entwined, to my apartment. He sees her first. Pulls me into the shadows. There is a moment of fear. Then excitement. I watch her—I see her—she doesn't see me.

"Does she always wear red?" I repeat. Brian barely hears me. His forehead is creased. Is there excitement for him, still? Or only fear?

"Not always," he says, finally. Hand on my ass, then between my legs. If there was fear, there is now only excitement. "But it is her favourite colour."

She's beautiful. And I... I do have this thought: this man, with a wife *like* that, wants me.

And it makes me feel good.

Feeling wanted always does.
—Yes.

Hiding in the archway, however, does not. And as we emerge from it, and continue our walk—and continue our afternoon (so very, very rarely do we get a night) in my bed—the feeling of distaste at the hiding, the ugliness of that moment, stays with me.

He works so very hard, but I don't come. And I don't relish his cock in my mouth, at all. For the first time, I feel... tainted.

But. It passes.

The third time I see Zia, she is in red, again. Well, sort of. She is wearing a red feather boa and nothing else. Splayed in the middle of Brian's—her—fuck, *their*—bed.

I scream, and run out of the bedroom. Out of the house.

That should have been the end. But of course, it's not.

25

On the way out, I knock over a little table in the hallway. I don't notice. I find out later it's what Zia's wedding bouquet—professionally dried, in pride of place as one entered Zia and Brian's house—stood on. Zia relishes the symbolism when she tells the story—to me. To her daughter. To anyone who will listen.

I know—because Annie tells me—that she gathers up the pieces, and takes them with her when she moves out.

To trash and burn? Or to reassemble and keep in a shrine in her new house?
—I don't know. I don't ask. I don't want to know the little Annie tells me.
And do you place your wedding bouquet in pride of place of the house of which you are about to become... what word shall I use? Mistress?
—Fuck. No. I have no idea what became of mine. I don't even know, I can't remember what it looked like. I had asked Brian to choose it. He defaulted to Annie's taste and judgement. So. It probably looked a lot like Zia's.
Twisted.
—A little.

So is this: Annie, maid of honour to Zia at the time of her marriage to Brian, wife of Brian's brother, essentially organizes our wedding. From the beginning, she is determined to love me. To be my "sister." I don't understand it, I don't know how she thinks she can manage it: to keep her friendship with Zia and to create one with me.

I would call her on it. But I don't know how.

"I am so happy we will be sisters!" she whispers in my ear at the wedding as she hugs me and kisses my cheek.

But she is the self-professed best friend of my husband's ex-wife. Well, and her ex-sister-in-law. What the fuck is she thinking?

She thinks… feeling wanted and loved always feels good.
—But I don't want her to love me.
No. I see that. So. Zia. The woman who always wore red. And Elizabeth…
—At this point, Zia calls me the whore who wore turquoise.
Oh. I love it. Tell me about it. Whore.

THE WHORE
WHO WORE TURQUOISE

FORGET LIPSTICK ON the collar. What betrays lovers is
lint. A piece of thread. Zia finds out about Brian and me—
so she yells at me a few months later—when she finds
turquoise thread snagged on his shirt button. Then
turquoise thread in the dryer lint trap.

I wear, at the time, affectedly and constantly, a fringed
turquoise silk scarf. The hedonist and sensualist in Brian
loves it. It is one of our favourite props. "I wish you didn't
already have this, so I could buy it for you," he whispers
when he tears it off me, puts it on me.

*Be more specific, lover of mine. How did he put it on?
What did he use it for? You know these are the things I
want to hear.*
—It's not important to the story.
*A scarf wound around a throat, a wrist, soaked with the
smell of sex, is always important to the story.*
—He did not use it the way you would.
*No, I imagine not. And now, I resent you for not wearing a
scarf today. Here. Take that stocking off. Yes. Now
continue, while I find things to do with it.*

It's all talk, of course. He never would buy it for me: he never buys me anything. He can't—or doesn't dare. Zia goes over every bill, line by line. Demands an accounting of every cash withdrawal from the ATM. I don't know this at the time—these are all details I learn during the divorce.

At the time, when my fog of lust starts to clear, I do notice that Brian is… cheap. That our rare hotel room days are always expensed conferences. That he only picks up the cheque when all I've ordered is an appetizer…

We play with the scarf—everywhere. In his office. In his car. And, extra stupidly, after we get too comfortable, in his house. He takes me on the desk in his "study"—no home office for this London-educated professor whose secret reading vice is Agatha Christie, no, it's a study, and I'm still so in lust I think it's sophisticated and sexy, rather than pretentious.

Eventually, the scarf makes its way to their bed.

Criminally stupid. I realize it then, I can't forgive it even now.

"That was incredibly idiotic," I tell him, the first time we fuck in their bedroom. It's not planned. We run into the house to pick up something. I don't wait in the car. Why? Curiosity? Maybe. We make out in the study. Fuck in the study, on the desk.

Oh, yes…

And then, "Do you want to see my bedroom?" "Oh yes." The bed.

Fuck.

Stupid.

Unforgivable.

The scarf leaves its evidence. Everywhere. Not on the sheets. Brian washes and dries the sheets—replaces them. It excites him—he tells me. He wants me in his bed again. He likes thinking of me when he's with his wife.

He likes pretending he can smell me on the sheets.

I should be appalled. I'm turned on.

As am I. Unforgivable. Hot.

And the scarf continues to leave its evidence.

Is Zia immediately suspicious when she notices the first turquoise thread? Or does it take until the tenth? The hundredth? I don't know, exactly: I do know that by the time she pulls out the tray of lint from the dryer, and there they are, woven through the lint, a tapestry of betrayal, she's actively looking for evidence.

"He washed the sheets, of course," she jeers. "He didn't think to clean out the lint trap."

I don't know what to say to that. I can't figure out how turquoise in the lint trap made her think... affair. I don't understand how a stray turquoise thread on Brian's coat, Brian's shirt, sent her hunting for more.

I don't understand love. Jealousy.

Yet.
—Yes.

"You were the only person I had ever seen him with who wore turquoise," she tells me later. "I remembered—you wore it when he introduced us. Don't you remember? You wore it to every fucking class. Once I saw... I knew who it was. And once I knew... it was only a matter of time before I caught you."

I don't understand.

"I knew you were fucking him the moment I saw how you looked at him," she says, bitterly.

Did she read all of that in that first encounter? During that tepid handshake, that introduction: "Zia, meet Elizabeth, one of our grad students. Elizabeth, my wife, Zia."

I wanted him, so badly, then.

But by the time Zia finds out about us, by the time she's finding threads, and by the time she sneaks back into the house to spring her trap in the bedroom while we're fucking in Brian's study, I'm trying to find a way to stop, to leave.

I'm done, although I'm too young and inexperienced to know it.

I'm also too young to know how to end it.

Have you gotten better at that, my Elizabeth?
—Oh yes. It's always over now, the first time I feel done.
Are you done with me?
—I'm still here, aren't I? But that is what my mistake of a marriage to Brian teaches me. To know, when I begin, that I'm just passing through. That it's temporary, and I'm not going to be fettered, caught.
Challenge accepted.
—Gauntlet not thrown down.
Totally thrown down. But I realize I'm the last—latest, do you prefer that word, my lover?—piece of a long chain. I think that must be the next part of the story—my predecessors, I mean. How quickly does the adulterer's new wife—the whore in turquoise—become an adulteress? And does she fuck her lovers in that same scarf?
—I burn the scarf. And I know you like the whore fantasy... but what really happens... fuck. I think it's defensive adultery.
Defensive adultery? I can't wait to hear you explain that... But first. Tell me this. You don't want him. You know this

31

already. So what the fuck happens? Why do you marry this man, anyway?
—Guilt.

Zia moves out, the day after her "discovery." And, of course, takes Destiny with her... but comes back, every day, to scream at Brian. So Brian tells me. I am his only solace, he says.

Funny thing, though. He sure as fuck doesn't want me any more than I want him. He wants his wife and daughter back. He doesn't say that. But he acts it. I know it. But I let him come to me, listen.

I let him fuck me.

And one day, when he calls me, tears and exhaustion in his voice, lonely, so lonely, so broken and asks me to come to the house, I do.

It's stupid.

It ruins my life.

But I do. And so I'm there, in that bedroom—it will soon be my bedroom, our bedroom, fuck, no—when we hear the door. Stomping. I stay in the room. But I hear... too much. First just sounds... and then more and more words. Brian's voice is just a murmur in the background. But Zia's... Christ. She screams, rails. Says such horrible, horrible things...

Such horrible things that at first, I have this thought— you fucking cunt, you bitch, you psychopath, no wonder he's cheating on you—I will remember that thought, that moment, with gut-wrenching shame when I find out about Brian's next grad student.

And then... she says more. Such horrible things, accusations, that I am sick to my stomach. Frozen. I need to be gone. I want this to be over. How did this happen? When will it end?

32

It ends. Not soon enough. A new pitch, a new volley of venom. My fault, all of it.

And then:

"Come on, Destiny. Fuck you, Brian."

A door slams.

I hear a slow, heavy tread on the stairs. I don't go out to meet him. I am sick. Horrified. Enveloped by nausea so intense I can barely see.

Brian stands before me, head bowed.

"Your daughter," I croak out. "Your daughter heard all that? She said all that, in front of your daughter?"

He says nothing, doesn't even nod his head. Reaches for me. I flinch away.

"Not right now," I say. "Not right now."

I spend the night with my back turned to him, as far away from him on the bed as possible, enveloped in self-hate.

Years later, I will realize this is my point of no return: the moment at which I decide I will have to marry him.

He asks me later. But not much later—I don't think the divorce is quite finalized. And when he asks me, I am aware of… Fuck. I am aware that I don't want to. He asks me in bed, one hand cupped around my breast, the other separating my cunt lips, so carefully, so carefully—with a promise of more. I spread my legs to invite his fingers to come inside. But they don't. He teases and tantalizes me. I relax, open, yearn.

"You will marry me, won't you, sweetheart?" his cajoling voice in my ear. My horror. I'm 25. About to start my career—a brilliant career, I am so fucking determined it will be a brilliant career, and I don't want to be tied to—to this man who's already crossed his peak, who I know is as high up as he's ever going to climb unless I shove him higher, and I don't want to be his helpmeet, his shadow.

I don't want to be his wife.

I don't want to be a fucking stepmother!

I just want... I just wanted...

You just wanted to fuck your law school professor.
—Yeah. For a while...

But I ruined his marriage. His life. I'm the reason his daughter won't talk to him, and his colleagues look at him funny.

There's only one way to make that up to him.

I don't fully articulate any of this to myself for years.

And, his mouth on my neck, his fingers probing inside me, the physical pleasure.

If I say yes, I will have this for the rest of my life, I think. That's not so bad, I think.

I'm 25. Naïve and stupid.

I say yes.

CARELESS

UGH. UGLY. FUCKING depressing.

—True.

Out of character. I cannot imagine the woman I fuck acting like that.

—I would not act like that now. But... yeah. That is how I acted, thought then.

So. No happily-ever-after for Brian and Zia. And what happens to Brian's attempt at happily-ever-after, take two?

We're not... unhappy. I am so wracked with guilt, I try really, really hard. The alpha veneer wears off Brian for me quickly, too quickly—I don't buy into the sage teacher persona, I see the holes in the logic and the inability to engage in really deep thought, the fact that he is more performer than intellectual—but the mechanics still work. We fuck constantly. His fingers, cock, tongue know how to play me, and play me enthusiastically.

I don't love him and I know I don't love him. But I say it all the time, and he doesn't know I don't love him. Does he love me? It matters, I suppose, as little as that I don't love him: we are stuck together.

So I suppose it's inevitable that we decide to make a child.

Yes. Children make everything easier. I've heard that.
—Don't be an asshole.
But I am. Still. I apologize, lover of mine. I don't mean to hurt your feelings. But I find this fascinating. Two intelligent people—I know you're discounting Brian's intelligence against your own, but I like him. I like how he seduced you. I like how he tethered you and trapped you. That takes skill. Power. Determination. So. With all that—two people like you. Making such a stupid decision.
—There is, I think, very little that's rational about marriage… And the decision to reproduce? Completely irrational. On every level. But worth it.
I've heard that too. I prefer not to find out, myself. Now. You said something about defensive adultery. Tell me that happens before you have a baby.
—Not exactly.

People like Brian and me don't reproduce spontaneously. No accidental pregnancies for us. I start eating the right things and go on pre-natal vitamin supplements before we ditch the birth control and Brian starts coming almost exclusively inside my vagina.

The poor man.
—He complains, a little. He misses oral sex. Anal sex, even more.
Who would not miss splitting this luscious ass?

I'm young enough that it doesn't take very long. Getting pregnant, I mean. And I find out that he's fucking around on me the same day—the same hour, almost—that I confirm I'm pregnant.

I suspect—the pregnancy, not the affair—for a few days. I feel… just different. And finally, my period is late, one day, two, seven. I run to a pharmacy on my way to the firm, and pee on a stick at lunch. Really? Really? I'm not sure I trust it, is it that easy? On the way home, I pick up another pregnancy test. Waltz into the house; run directly to the bathroom.

Two minutes. And…

I pirouette through the hallway. Into Brian's study; he should be home. And there's evidence that he is—or has been there—a stack of term papers on his desk, leaning a little, like a mini-tower of Pisa.

"Brian?" I call out. I can't wait to tell him. I am happy, and I am young and stupid, and I do see, around the corner, a happily-ever-after of sorts—the two of us, arm-in-arm, pushing a stroller…

"Upstairs!" his voice. "On the phone with Annie! Coming right down!"

It's either the bang of the door closing behind him or the air draft created by his entrance that causes the Tower of Pisa of term papers to come crashing down to the floor.

"Oh, fuck," he says, and we are both on our knees, gathering them up. "Just leave it, Liz, I'll do it," he says, and he scoops them up. And it's as he lifts them up, in an untidy pile, onto his desk, that a single sheet of paper escapes from the pile and falls at my feet.

It's one of those thick, faux-hand-made papers stationery stores sell at extortionate prices, and it's filled with large, round, almost childish writing, in hot pink—of course, what else—ink. And I'd think nothing of it, perhaps, as I bend to pick it up, except that Brian flushes and drops the rest of the papers to the floor again.

"Give me that," he snatches at it, and so, I evade him. I stand there, holding the sheet of paper in my hand, and I feel sick. "Give that to me, Liz," he says. "It's personal."

"Don't fucking call me Liz," I say. My hand is sweating; I know my fingerprints are smearing into the paper, into the letter.

"Elizabeth," his voice, pleading.

If I don't look, I won't find out. I won't know.

If Zia hadn't sought to find out, to reveal—Brian and I would have petered out and ended. And the disaster of our marriage, of this life I now have bound to this weak, frustrating man, would have been averted.

Fuck. I close my eyes.

Except. I don't have to look to know. Why is Brian such a fucking terrible liar?

I drop the letter to the floor without looking at it. Turn around and walk out of the room, and out of the house, without looking at Brian.

I'm not thinking. At all. I'm on some kind of bizarre autopilot so I'm not quite sure how I end up at the airport. And then on an airplane to Montréal.

Canada's sexiest city. Except before you get there, you fuck a pilot in the cockpit…
—How much porn do you watch?
Not that much, really. I prefer to live it. Anyway. Continue. You find out your adulterous husband is, again, an adulterer. What do you do?

REVENGE SEX

I DO KNOW what—who—I'm going to do when I land in Montréal. Pierre-André. A law school classmate. A former lover. Charming. Slutty. Morally impaired. Guaranteed to be available, even if he is at the time nominally attached.

The flight attendant asks me if I want coffee and I weep. Why? Because I'm so cliché, again. And this is so lame. And just as I did not want to be Elizabeth the home-wrecker— how did I become that?—I don't want to be Elizabeth the divorcée. But I suppose. I could do that. I could do that. Except, there is a baby growing inside me.

I don't know what to do.

I don't want to be a single mom.

I don't want to be Zia.

I don't want to be me, either.

My poor lover.
—You mock me.
No, no. I see it. Palpable drama. I wonder how much of it you are creating in retrospect.
—None of it. That is how I felt.
And yet, as you tell me the story, my hand nestled between your legs tells me you're wet and aroused. By the mention of Pierre-André?
—Perhaps merely by your hand between my legs.

A woman's most responsive sex organ is her brain—as all good lovers know. So something about the story pleases you. What? Anticipating revenge sex with the Frenchman?
—I don't know. The revenge sex was terrible.
No? Really? Let me make that up to you, a little. Don't let your hands idle while your mouth talks. On with the story…

I suppose Pierre-André picks me up at the airport. I don't recall. And then I'm in his condo. And on his bed, naked. I think I actually say, "I fucking hate my husband right now, and I need to fuck." He probably says nothing, just takes off his clothes. And mine.

He had been one of my… no, hands down, my favourite, my best lover before Brian. The worst possible boyfriend. But an unparalleled lover. So good at taking—just a little more than I wanted to give. So good at giving—just a little less than I wanted… and then more, fuck, more, stop! But not stopping… That day, as I lie there beneath him, there is no taking or giving. There is just the grinding of genitals, and I am barely present, and it is awful.

Like… really awful. There he is, thrusting in and out of me, and I can't figure out why it's so bad. Maybe it's the panting. Maybe it's the droplets of sweat pooling on his temples, his damp hair? Maybe it's because I no longer like the way he smells? I sigh and stretch, to get a little more comfortable under him. Fail. But he takes that as a signal of pleasure, and murmurs, "You like that, baby? You still like that?" and does whatever it is that he's doing again—what is he doing? Nothing, nothing that matters. In and out, in and out. I'd get more fucking pleasure from a dildo. I let myself think that Brian's really good in bed.

Readjust again.

And starting grinding my hips against his to bring the entire icky episode to a faster close.

Shall I ask you to consider whether you were just not in the mood? Or did Brian spoil you for other lovers?

—I don't know. There is something in the idea that my standard of what made a good lover when I was 20 and my standard of what made a good lover ten years later were quite different... And yes. Brian knew how to fuck. And yes. He set the bar high.

And he trained you well. I... ah... so appreciate it. So. You decide to stay with him for the sex?

—Christ. Of course not.

As Pierre-André finally comes, and his sweat and smell cover me, and tears well up in my eyes—and he thinks it's from my orgasm, and has a story to tell himself and his buddies, "I fucking made her cry!"—I try to make myself think. What am I going to do? What should I do? Is this an out? Is this karma? Is this my just desserts?

The baby in my belly complicates everything.

And I can't think.

I let Pierre-André fuck me again in the morning. I tell him I need him to be brutal and selfish; that I want to hurt and cry and feel the evidence of the fucking for days to come, and he gets hard immediately...

Fuck, yeah. Me too...

...and does his best, but it's not good enough. He does not fuck me into oblivion, much less enlightenment. I waddle through airport security unsated and unhappy. And arrive back in Calgary without a clue as to what I'm going to do.

I don't know what I'm going to do even as I go home. I go home—to Brian's house—because I don't know where else to go.

The door's open, which is good, as I left without my keys. I hear voices in the kitchen... and I think about evading them. Should I maybe go upstairs? Just go into the bedroom, pack, and go to a hotel, and then the next day, look for an apartment...

"Elizabeth!" It's Brian. He runs towards me, arms outstretched, and before I know what is happening, he has me in an embrace. "Elizabeth! My love! Thank god!"

I am rigid and I don't want him to hold me. I don't want him to think I've come back. I haven't!

"Dad?" Sasha—she is still Destiny—follows him into the hallway.

She is almost ten, but so very small.

She wraps herself around Brian's leg. Hides her face in his untucked shirt tail.

"I just picked her up," he says. "Annie called me, she was with her. Zia..." his voice trails off. Destiny punches him and stomps her feet.

"Don't talk about my mother to her!" she screams. And runs up the stairs, crying.

He just picked her up. Annie called him. Zia...

He doesn't need to tell me more.

I step away from him.

"We're having a baby," I say. I cut off his attempt to... what? Congratulate me? Us? "We're having a baby, and our baby will have a functioning nuclear family," I say.

"Elizabeth, beloved, I'm so happy... let me explain..." he moves towards me. I move back.

"I don't fucking want to hear it," I say. "I don't fucking want to hear it. Just... fuck. Be discrete. Don't rub it in my face. Don't..."

"Elizabeth," another step forward. "Liz. My love. You have to know that... I would never... You are the only one..."

His silver tongue is not functioning, there are only sentence fragments, and he doesn't believe them even as he says them. As he speaks, anger builds inside me. Such burning, explosive anger that when it comes out of me, if I speak, our marriage will be over.

And it can't be, because there is a baby in my belly who needs a family. And a little girl crying upstairs who needs to be protected.

Protected?
—Protected.

"Don't fucking rub it in my face," I repeat. Turn away from him and start walking up the stairs. I stop three steps up, turn around. Look at him with loathing and contempt I can't hide. "And Brian? Never in our fucking house, in our fucking bed. Do you understand?"

I turn my back on him and don't hear his response. Go up the stairs.

But I stay.

You stay, to be unhappy.
—I stay, to be a mother.
And stepmother.
—Well. Like I said before... I don't think out the implications of that very well.

RENAMING DESTINY

I WONDER HOW many affairs, how many divorces wouldn't happen if people really understood how awful it is to have stepchildren. What a mindfuck of a role it is, to be a parent-not-a-parent.

I still wonder if, had I been sane enough to realize that Brian was a father, if I would have not... but it doesn't matter. I did. And so. Here I am, a stepmother, with a stepdaughter who hates me.

The stepdaughter who shares your daughter's name...
—What?
Sasha is the diminutive form of Alexandra. Your biological daughter's name in this story. As you won't tell me the real one. Coincidence or are you playing with facts for storytelling effect?
—What do you think?
So clever, so deceitful, so effective. Lay back, spread your legs, and take a short break while I reward your creativity. And then explain.
—Oh. Fuck. Yes. All right...

When I entered—shattered—her life, she was still Destiny. Of course, Zia would name her child something ridiculous like Destiny. It could have been worse—Brian would tell me, at some point, that the names bandied about included Love, Eternity, Promise, and Purity. Their boy— "Thank god we did not have a son!"—was going to be a slightly less blasphemous version of Seed of Allah or Messiah.

Jesus or Mohammed bandied about too?
—No.
Of course not, what was I thinking. Too obvious, not symbolic enough.

Brian calls her Dez, a small act of rebellion, perhaps, because Zia relentlessly corrects him. "Destiny, Destiny!"

The first real conversation Destiny and I have is about her name.

She is in our house on a Daddy weekend, locked in her bedroom, crying and screaming, the pitch of her voice so much like Zia's I want to vomit. But I knock. Knock harder. She opens the door and screams at me.

"I hate it, hate it, hate it! I hate it! Why did she do this to me? I hate it! I hate her! I hate you!"

I think… she's talking about the divorce. And perhaps on some level she is. But on the level that matters in that moment, she's talking, crying about her name.

"Change it," I say. I'm standing in the doorway of her bedroom. Awkward. Uninvited. Not belonging. Unconnected. It's been three years since we've been thrust into each other's lives. We're still aliens. She hates me. I don't know what to do with her.

"Change it," I repeat. Offering a solution when, most likely, what's needed is an embrace, a kiss. Empathy. The comfort of a loving parent.

Which I'm not.

I am a terrible stepmother. She's not the most awesome stepdaughter, granted. But she is entitled to be bitter, angry, resentful, and I have no right to complain.

I don't love her.

It's not intentional.

I don't know children at all when she comes into my life. She is five and confused and terrified. I am confused and terrified. And so I fuck up. I maintain distance, give her space.

Send her, with every act, every word, spoken and not, the message that I am not her parent.

Maybe my excuse is that she does not want me to be her parent: she has a father, a mother. And Annie, a godmother who loves her so ardently I think it distasteful, almost obscene. But the truth is I'm not interested. I don't know how. I don't want to learn. I tell myself I have no rights and I do everything I can to remain on the periphery of her life.

So. Instead of comfort, I offer a solution.

"Change it," I repeat. "Your Dad calls you Dez. Your friends call you Dez." The sobs increase. I know, in that moment, because I know girls, where the tears are coming from. Her friends call her Dez—except when they call her "Des-tee-nee!"

"Change it," I repeat. "Change your name. You can choose..." My voice trails off. I swear I did not intend to say "choose your destiny," but I think we both hear those words—in Zia's dramatic delivery, no less.

She sobs out, between gasps of tears, that it won't work. That everyone knows her as Destiny. That's what they call her, will call her. They do it, all the time, to tease, torment. Dez, when they want something from her. Destiny *("Des-tee-nee!")* when they want to hurt.

"Don't respond," I tell her. She rolls her eyes. I'm the stupid adult, the robot, who knows nothing.

"Do you know how many different nicknames an Elizabeth can have?" I ask her. We rattle them off. All the worst ones. Lizzie. Betty. Bet! El-*ai*-za!

"I am none of those," I tell her. "I am Elizabeth."

"Dad calls you Liz," she ventures. It's my turn to roll my eyes.

"I think he does that because it's almost an anagram for Zia," I tell her. Then immediately wish I hadn't; it seems too intimate a revelation, too much like something Zia might tell her about me.

I call you Liz, sometimes. Do you mind?
—Not from you.
Good. Liz-lover-of-mine.

And then, I lie. I make up a heartening story about how I went to kindergarten as Betty—because my mother, clearly, loved *Archie* comics as a child but hated me, or at least had no forethought—no, she *hated* me.

"Imagine what my classmates did with that," I tell Destiny.

"I wonder if the same thing happens to Veronicas," she says. Wipes her nose.

"I don't know," I say. Ponder. "Probably not. Veronica's hot, a hard-ass. Betty's insipid. A victim. Chasing a boy who doesn't want her, who's so not worth it." I refuse to entertain that I've just voiced a metaphor. I tell her I rechristen myself Elizabeth abruptly, after hiding and crying in a stall in the girls' washroom for two hours one day.

"Really?" she asks. I see her imagining me crying.

"Really," I lie, but not really, because I did hide and cry in a stall in the girls' washroom for two hours, more, and not just once, and while it wasn't because of my name, it was because of my mother.

My rechristening is obnoxious, relentless, I tell her. I correct one and all. "My name is Elizabeth." Then, I stop responding to calls for "Betty" altogether. Not from teachers, not from friends. Certainly not from tormentors.

"It took two years," I tell her. And she's appalled.

"Two years?" She's eight and a half. Two years? That's an eternity.

"Two years. But no one has called me Betty since."

I see the thought in her eyes almost before she's aware she's had it. She may hate her name, and I am offering her succor, sort of—but she really hates me. I step across the threshold of the room, into her bedroom, stepping aggressively into her space, for the first time in our joint lives. I kneel down beside her bed, so my eyes are at the level of hers.

"If you want to change your name," I say, "today, tomorrow, ten years from now, I will support you. Fully. As in, we change it on all your legal documents. And in this house, you will never be Destiny again." I pause. Catch her red-rimmed eyes and hold them.

"But if you ever call me Betty, in anger, or as a joke, I will come into this room and strip it of everything—*everything*—except the fitted sheet on the mattress. And I will make every single one of your evil stepmother fantasies come true. And then some."

I am a terrible, terrible stepmother.

I walk out of her bedroom, slowly. Close the door—gently.

Wonder what will happen next.

Nothing does. Nothing changes. She still hates me. I still don't love her. Her name is still Destiny.

She never calls you Betty, though.
—No. Nor Liz.

And then, two years later, a week or two after Alexandra is born, Destiny comes into my bedroom—our bedroom, Brian's and mine, formerly her parents bedroom, Jesus, why, why did I move into this house? I'm in bed with Alexandra, madly under-slept, trying to ram my nipple into her reluctant, adorable little mouth. But I'm also happy, so perfectly happy in a cloud of oxytocin-induced euphoria and "I made this miracle" bliss.

Enter Destiny.

She stands in the doorway of the bedroom. At its threshold.

So many mirrors and parallels in your stories.
—Life is one big fucking cliché. It's really quite embarrassing.

"Remember when you said if I decided to change my name, you'd support me, completely," she asks.

I remember. Nod.

"I'm ready," she says. "I want my new name to be Sasha."

"OK," I say. The fogginess of my baby-brain diffuses—disarms the intent, if there was such, of her sting—I don't notice it, actually. It's Brian who points out to me that Sasha could be a diminutive form of Alexandra. It's Annie who wonders, politely, indirectly, awkwardly, if that's really a good idea.

It's Zia, mistress of the multi-pronged emotional attack, who demands, at the top of her lungs as I'm trying to get Alexandra to sleep, whether "Sasha" was my idea and my attempt to exercise dominion over her daughter—to erase her rightful name and give her one of my choosing.

"It's not enough that you steal my husband, you have to steal, rename my daughter, too?" she howls.

"Fuck you," I tell her. And, to Brian, "Get your ex-wife the fuck out of our house. Now." He doesn't—I'm the one to leave, the study if not the house.

When Alexandra is six weeks old, *en route* to her second post-natal check-up, I stop at the registry office, my stepdaughter in tow, to officially, legally change Destiny's name to Sasha.

The stepdaughter and daughter motif disturbs me. Perhaps because I am an evolutionary dead-end and cannot fully relate. Also, there is a distinct unpleasantness to the idea that the naked woman at my feet is a mother. With feelings, responsibilities I cannot fathom. Greater uses, an actual social purpose other than as the repository of my cock in her various tempting openings...

—All of those parts make up me. Make up any woman who has had children.

Just because something is, and is inevitable, doesn't mean I have to like it.

—I guess that's the way I feel about having Sasha in my life too. And her mother. Inevitable. But I don't have to like it.

And Annie?

—I don't understand why I have to have her in my life at all. But she's there, she's always fucking there...

DREAMING OF SILENCE

THE PREGNANCY'S EASY and uncomplicated, and Brian so consumed by guilt that he is a perfect, attentive expectant father. Comes to all the appointments. Rubs my feet and back when I come home from work. Cooks, shops for groceries, loads the dishwasher.

Buys all sorts of ridiculous baby things I don't want, we don't need. I accept it all, calmly. It soothes me. I think, it will be all right. Everything will be all right.

And when Alexandra is born…

You're not going to describe the fucking birth, are you? Because that's beyond buzz kill.
—No. Do you want to hear the story or not?
Talk. But skip the parts you know I don't want to hear.

…when Alexandra is born, and I see him holding her, and he's happy, and I'm fucking ecstatic, and she's so beautiful… I again think some version of happily-ever-after might be possible. She is here, she is beautiful, and we are a family.

Except, of course, we are just three parts of a bigger, messier family.

I don't realize until much, much later that of course Alexandra's birth and the increased frequency of Zia and

Brian screaming matches at our house are related. At the time, in a baby fog, I am barely aware of time, much less cause.

But I spend a lot of time dreaming of silence, of which there isn't a lot.

Instead, there is a lot of this: Zia arrives. Often with Sasha. Sends Sasha upstairs… or holds onto her hand, tightly, while she starts discussing. Something. A situation at school. A field trip? Report card. Money. The topic is irrelevant. Soon, there is screaming, emoting, pounding on the table. And Brian tries to… ineffectual, always, but, trying, I admit, always, trying… he tries to soothe her.

Annie, inevitably, shows up. Why? Sometimes, she arrives with Zia—or shortly thereafter, to get Sasha, take her away—Zia must call her when she's on her way. Sometimes Zia interrupts the screaming to call her: "They're ganging up on me! I need you here to take my side!" Sometimes Brian says, "You know, we need an impartial person to help us through this, let me call Annie," and Zia always agrees, and sometimes, there is silence—heavy breathing—while we wait for Annie's arrival.

Me? Before Alexandra is born, I stand there, awkward, silent. I bear witness to Brian and Zia's arguments, grit my teeth at Zia's accusations, ignore Brian's pleas for succor. How can I take a side? How can I possibly have a voice? I shouldn't even be there… I won't even sit down in a chair, preferring to perch at the threshold of the door, ready to bolt, to withdraw.

The scenes invariably take place in Brian's study.

The place where he takes you on his desk.
—That was before we were married.
Fucking marriage. Ruins everything.

The study in no way hints at the sensualist and hedonist within Brian. It's all law professor, and conventional law professor at that. There are bookcases double-and-triple stacked with books he does not always read but has to have. A large desk. Before the room becomes the primary setting for never-ending family drama, my favourite part of it is the little round table in its darkest corner, half-hidden by shadows. I sit there, after we fuck, and watch him re-arrange his desk, and his clothes.

Yourself still in disarray, legs spread, watching him watching you. You enjoy that part of the post-coital experience, much too much.
—Yes. I'm surprised you noticed.
I notice everything.

Over the desk—a hanging, stained-glass lamp I once loved. Around it, three chairs, comfortable but sleek.

There were always three chairs—in case he was entertaining two colleagues, or fantasizing about seducing two TAs simultaneously. But at some point post-divorce, both Brian and Zia come to believe the three chairs represent Sasha's three "parents." Brian believes this in a simple—stupid, naïve—"look at us, doing our best for our daughter," 21st century modern family way. Zia holds it as an affront, an abomination, certain the third seat is an intentional humiliation. And, my idea, of course.

She doesn't notice that most of the time, it is she, Brian, and Annie in the chairs—while I hover on the periphery, inching my way towards the door... wondering if I can escape.

The first time I break my silence, I am sitting in one of the chairs, nursing Alexandra—she's barely two, three months old—and I am under-slept, exhausted, and done,

done with this circus. I can't remember what Zia is upset about, what she's agitating for anymore… maybe it's about Destiny's name change, maybe it's about a school suspension… but I do remember I call Zia a "psychotically controlling fucking cunt."

As in, "Maybe if you weren't such a psychotically controlling fucking cunt, she would not need to rebel so fucking often! Fuck!"

"Liz!" this from Brian. "The baby!"

"Yes, the baby!" I scream. Zia-style, and so I'm immediately ashamed, and even as I yell, I promise myself that this first time will be the last time—I will never do this again. "I should be paying attention to the baby. Or sleeping. Not listening to yet another venomous attack by your bitter cunt of an ex-wife who still hasn't moved on, and who blames me for everything. You know what? I blame me too. I shouldn't have fucked Brian. God knows I didn't want to marry Brian. But here I am, and here we all are, so suck it up, and take some responsibility for something. And try to just—here's an idea—just fucking try listening to your daughter sometime. Just fucking try that for five fucking minutes."

Ouch.

And, *my* daughter at my breast, I exit the room.

Do you keep your promise?
—What?
Do you keep your promise, to yourself? That this first time is the last time?
—I try. I try so fucking hard.

54

BABY OIL

I'M CURLED AROUND Alexandra, inhaling her baby scent and hiding from the world, when Brian walks quietly into the room.

"I'm sorry," he says as he sits down on the bed. I don't move or acknowledge him. "I'm sorry," he says again, and climbs onto the bed. Spoons me.

"I do know," he says. Pauses. "I do know how hard this is for you. How hard she is on you." I'm not sure if he's talking about Zia or Des… Sasha, now. I'm angry, hurt, exhausted—guilty, always, guilty—and I don't want to explore any of those feelings further. Not even in an apology.

His hands caress my back and neck. And because I'm curled around Alexandra and loving her, I am not rigid. The liquidity of my spine is a response and Brian's fingers build on it.

"Can I move the baby?" he whispers. I still don't speak. But I disengage from Alexandra and move towards him. He slips my T-shirt off me in one practiced move. Carefully caresses around my breasts, emptied now, but always a little sore. His hands trace lines and broad strokes down my hips, thighs. Across the not-taut-and-will-it-ever-be-again? belly.

I love those lines, marks on your belly, thighs.

—I do too. But it took me years to own them.
Let me show you how much I love those lines while you talk...

Then he slides me off the bed onto the yoga mat on the floor; grabs a pillow as we descend.

"On your stomach," he whispers. Growls. I take the pillow and slide it under my breasts. And then...

"What's that?"

"Baby oil," he says. "The mother of my child needs a massage, no?"

I have the thought that Zia is also the mother of his child. What does she need now? But I push it away and pay attention only to his fingers, hands, the smooth, silky feel of the baby oil on my neck, shoulders, back, arms. Ass. Thighs. Calves. Between my toes. Each stroke more relaxing and arousing than the last.

"Magic fingers," I murmur.

"Magic body," he murmurs back. He's straddling my thighs, and reaching under my pelvis to *that* part of the hips, the belly. The mound of my cunt. I moan, a little. Then stiffen.

"Still sore. Afraid," I say.

"OK." The fingers move away. Return to my ass. I feel a trickle of baby oil between my ass cheeks. And then a finger in my asshole. He strokes and stretches me and I focus on each individual moment and sensation. Is there going to be a cock in my ass?

There is. Now. Although I have to say, it's taking effort to maintain this erection.
—It's taking effort to tell you this part of the story.
All right. I commend your effort. Talk. I will imitate.

I steel myself. Relax into the fingers. And then, into the cock when it comes.

And with his fingers—"magic fingers," still—under me, stroking my clit, caressing the outside lips and mound, but never parting the lips or going inside, and his cock stroking in and out of me with uncharacteristic gentleness, I come. Quickly and silently, and I don't announce it; perverse in this moment, I don't want him to know. He comes just a few moments later. Apologetic.

"I'm sorry." Apparently, that's the thing he says today. "It's been so long. And your beautiful body excites me so much."

I remain still on my belly while he cleans the semen and baby oil off me, and then climb into the bed with him, both of us still naked. And I wrap myself around him, and try to sink into him, and he holds me. And that, I think, is our terrible mistake.

We fuck. It feels good. We pretend it's solved something. But of course, it never does.

In a bedroom down the hall, sleeps a teary-eyed Destiny—Sasha—left behind when her mother leaves—"I can't handle her right now!" —a little girl who doesn't want to be here and who resents my existence.

Somewhere across town, a wild-eyed Zia is crying. Screaming.

Maybe drinking.

Nothing is right with the universe.

But for a few minutes, as far as our bodies are concerned, nothing could be better.

I roll away from Brian and back towards Alexandra. And I would weep, but I don't know how.

It is telling of Brian's relationship not just to me, but to life, that he does not, that night, or ever again, refer—or even allude—to my statement that I should have never married him.

Surprisingly, Zia never takes advantage of the weapon I hand her either. Could she not have done cruel, cruel things with that? Had a new wife told me, "I didn't want to marry him, but here I am!" … oh, the things I could have done to her with that…

I can hear it…
—But, of course, I am determined not to be an ex-wife.
And you stay the course.
—I do. Although… I know that I detach more and more from Brian. I can't help it, I can't control it. It just happens.

SPERM DONOR

THERE IS A moment—it marks a milestone for me, I'm not sure if it does for him—when I effectively leave. Not physically, but emotionally—detach to the extent that were I to walk in on him in *our* bed with his grad student of the moment, I'd just shrug and tell them to change the fucking sheets after. I recognize it even at the time. It happens when Alexandra goes through a particularly clingy stage—when she's two, nearing three. She calls me "Pillow." First, "I need you, Mommy! You are my pillow!" Then, "Pillow! Pillow! Come to me, my-Pillow!" And I come to her, and she embraces me, and then kisses one breast and then the other (calls each her little-little pillow as she kisses them) and whispers, in incomprehensible Alexandra talk, profusions of love and adoration for her Pillow.

She can only fall sleep with her head on Pillow's breasts.

I am exhausted. But also exhilarated. I am so loved. I glow.

Brian is amused. And also...

"I feel so unnecessary," he says. He stands in our bedroom, where I am trapped on the bed, under Alexandra's head, attempting to review some papers for a client bitch session in the morning. "She doesn't need me, or want me, ever."

He doesn't add, "And neither do you," but it's implied.

"It's the age," I say. Vaguely. I'm distracted. Alexandra's sweaty head on my breasts. Papers all around me.

"It was the same with Destiny," he says.

"Sasha," I correct him, automatically. I am as vigilant about her new name as she is, maybe even more.

"She was Destiny, then," he says.

I say nothing.

"When she was born," he continues, "I felt so unnecessary. There were the two of them—and I was just the sperm donor."

On the tip of my tongue: Do. Not. Compare. Me. To. Zia.

And also: "Maybe that's all you are."

But I don't say it. I don't look at him. I keep my eyes on my papers.

He isn't finished.

"That's when I had my first affair, you know," he says. "When Destiny was... six months old? Zia and I hadn't had sex—any real interaction, really—other than 'Go pick up more diapers' in months. And so I... And I felt awful. So awful. So bad. And Zia... she didn't even notice."

I realize that he's telling me this for a reason. What does he hope to achieve? An offer, by me, to get Alexandra out of our bed, out of my arms, right now, so we can fuck? Absolution for the affair I know about, now more than three years old? The affairs in-between that I don't know about, that I don't notice, because I'm so wrapped up in Alexandra?

"Well," I say instead, and I speak with deliberation, an intention to hurt. "I guess it's good that you've gotten more practice at fucking around over the years. And that you started cheating on me well before Alexandra was born. Must make it easier now."

He leaves, silent, back bent.

I feel... nothing.
I realize it's possible to stay... and to leave, anyway.

Do you cry?
—What a stupid thing to say. Of course not.
Does he?
—I don't know. Maybe. I think... I think, until that moment, maybe we both thought, on some level, there would be a reconciliation of some sort. Instead... Fuck, instead, what do I do? I tell him, really, how much I don't need him. That he is unnecessary.
Except as a sperm donor.
—Those were his words. But yes. And I think... I don't know, because we never talk about it, but I think this is *the* conversation that sets the stage for the next eight years. It establishes... everything. My cynicism. His... "freedom." Our estrangement.
Dark.
—I know it sounds dark... But, see. There's Alexandra. And I am so in love with Alexandra, her father barely matters. He's right about that.
Fuck. I want to beat you on his behalf. Cold, cold bitch. How is your ass?
—Still sore.
Good. I will make it more sore. But tales of your motherly devotion are eroding my desire to fuck. Switch gears. Tell me about your next lover.
—It happens not long after this conversation, actually. My next lover, I mean. It's a client.
I like it already. You with a client.
—Whore fantasy.
Every man has one. The kick comes from thinking you can control your whore—and she loves only you.

ALWAYS THE WOMAN'S FAULT

IT'S SHORTLY THEREAFTER that I engage in the very criminal thought that while I demanded that Brian not fuck around in *our* bed, he made no such demand or request of me, and I am free to fuck around wherever the hell I want to. Including the marital bed.

Oh, yes...
—Down, lover. It is just a thought.

I don't, of course I don't. Because our bed is in our house which is Alexandra's house and... I can't, I won't.

In fact, with the exception of that immediate post-discovery fuck in Montréal with Pierre-André, pregnancy, lactation, and falling in love with the new life that I created—mine, she's mine, she came out of me, and she is mine!—ensure I am totally faithful. For years.

Sleeplessness, exhaustion, and lack of time and desire help.

So my first conscious affair doesn't take place until Alexandra is three, perhaps more.

You don't count the French Canadian as an affair because he was a one-off? Or so bad in bed?

—I don't count him as *conscious*. He was my revenge fuck. My "I'm not going to be a goddamn victim; I'm so not going to be Zia" reaction. Do you understand? Brian was going to fuck around? Fine. I was not going to be the cheated-upon, victim wife. I was going to fuck around too. But, it was all... unconscious. There was no thought, no decision, not really. Just action.

I think I understand. I am not fettered by marriage, of course, but I have occasionally been with women who think they have acquired an exclusive license on my cock. And I have let them think so... so I suppose in those cases, when I take another lover, I do cheat. But I prefer not to cheat out of anger. I try to be motivated purely by lust.

—I think, if I am honest, a tinge of anger fuels most of my affairs. Even this one. But even with that, and despite the way it ended, I'm still... I still remember most of it, very fondly. It was also my first really big professional win.

So. I am again a cliché, and my first conscious affair is a client. But with a life that consists of child-work-sleep, who else could it be? It will never be a colleague. The senior partner who's mentoring me ensures that during my articling year, before I go to grad school, before I meet Brian.

I'm 22, 23, and my "mentor" is almost three times my age. Sexist, racist. Cruel. Brilliant, and so I forgive him every barb; I mine his brain, his files, his assistant's ability to bridge two worlds and three generations.

He sees me having lunch, once, twice, three times, with one of the firm's up-and-coming stars. A securities lawyer, just this side of 30. Still an associate, but everyone's favourite. A big biller, a heavy-hitter—I think so, anyway. He speaks French, German, Italian. Has a family name with clout. A network, connections, personal relationships with several of the firm's top clients. Promises to introduce me to people. Suggests there are conferences and networking events we could go to together.

I'm not fucking him. But I'm not, as we lunch, and I look at his teeth, his hair, and listen to his voice, averse to the idea.

My mentor notices. *He* doesn't buy me lunch. Or coffee. He just dumps a pile of files on my desk and tells me to find a needle in a haystack. And, over his shoulder, as he walks away, tells me:

"Oh, and child? If you have any thoughts about sleeping your way to the top—accelerating your career by hitching it to a rising star? I'm not talking about myself—I'm done rising and unfortunately, there isn't enough Viagra in the world to make this old pole perform the way it would have to if I wanted to keep a little thing like you entertained—but there are others who… Humph, it happens all the time. Yes. And maybe you're not as bright as I think you are, and will decide to take a fucking short cut. You won't be the first. Or the last. But when the shit hits the fan—and it will, because the wife always finds out, the assistant always finks, the other jealous up-and-comer sees you playing footsie at a company function or coming out of the same hotel lobby— when the shit hits the fan, it's always the woman's fault.

"And she's the one who needs to be… humph… removed from the firm.

"It's always the woman's fault."

He pauses. Stares at me to make sure I get the message. My cheeks are red, but I'm meeting his eyes.

"Also, child? Don't confuse a facility with languages for mastery of the law. Or brains, really."

I'm, at that moment, in total denial that fucking my way to the top was at all in my thoughts. But I'm impressionable enough that, at the next coffee with my trilingual colleague, I notice that he's bland... in three languages.

Also, securities lawyer? How is that even a thing? I'm going to be a litigator.

My encounter with Brian in grad school makes me switch direction again, from criminal litigation—that's his beat— back to the more profitable area of business law. But, as a litigator determined to straddle both worlds.

I'm waiting for you to straddle your client.
—So impatient.
I am bored of the foreplay. On your fucking back and spread your legs. Ah. Now. Hurry. And skip all the technical legal details. I really don't give a fuck.
—All you need to know is that Company A needed to buy Company B without buying asset C...
What did I just say, cunt?
—Ha. Funny you should say *that*...

CUNT IN A BOARDROOM

IT'S MY FIRST overnight business trip since Alexandra's been born, and the impetus for it comes from two places. I have been careful—obsessively careful—to keep up my billable hours, to not let childbirth and motherhood knock me off the partner track. My sexist, racist, downright cruel mentor—to whom I return with an MLM and a law professor for a husband—tells me, when he sees the swell of my pregnant belly, "Breed if you must. But you know all that crap on our website about work-life balance, and extended parental leave, and support for diversity, bla bla bla? It's all lies." And I know he's right, so I outsource housework, laundry, meal preparation, and having a life, and all I do is love Alexandra, live on caffeine, and put in more hours than the hungriest, most ambitious male associate.

And I'm on the cusp of making partner, I know this… but I'm, maybe, a little young. And I have tits and no penis. And that still matters here.

I have a champion and mentor. And I haven't fucked it up by fucking him, or anyone else.

But I still need… a big win. And a client who will follow me anywhere. To do that, I need a high profile file. I need to roll the dice on something, risk big, win big. But while I've been clocking in the hours—I have not been taking centre stage.

Until—this file comes up. And it has a wrinkle. A messy technical wrinkle no one quite knows how to solve, and it's causing everyone—including my mentor who's the senior partner on the file—angst.

I don't know how to solve it either, but I sink into it. And I keep all the pieces in my head. And I'm essential to the file. And I must go to Houston to present our attempt to iron out the wrinkle—I don't even have to ask. My mentor commands it. "I need your memory," he says.

More than adequate motivation. But there's more?

I am... restless. I am exhausted and under-slept and still so-in-love with Alexandra. But. I am restless. I want to be away.

You want to play.
—Maybe...

I don't confess that to myself until I am on the plane. And I'm so excited. To be away, to be in the game.

I drown myself in the data on the flight, even though we have a game plan and a strategy and an agreement in principle to present.

We completely fuck it up...

Where the fuck's the point at which you meet the client?
—He picks us up at the airport and we pow-wow in the car on the way to the meeting. But you see... he doesn't matter, not at that point. There are no fireworks, no immediate chemistry. He only matters, at that point, as the client—or the representative of the client, really. He's not even that important—he's not the CEO or a real vice-president. He's a VP

Legal—the General Counsel. A captive in-house lawyer. The most important thing, really, is that his job is on the line if this deal goes sideways. And it does. We fuck it up.

Or, to be more precise, the client and my senior partner fuck it up. The other side comes out all guns blazing and shoots down our proposal to iron out that wrinkle, knocks them off-kilter, and they don't know how to respond. Our agreement in principle, a decent, win-win (almost) way of solving the problem is replaced by a "we're bigger so we're gonna fuck you in the ass and you're going to say thank you" Texan approach.

Speaking off... roll over...
—I need my breath.
I'll use a lot of lube, it won't hurt much... this time.

It's a massacre and it's surreal. I have this sense of... it's psychological warfare, really. It's not law. It's the way Brian would argue a case, I think, and as soon as I think that, I see the flaw. I see where *they* fucked up. And I see—I see what we haven't seen before. I see how we can win. Totally.

"Excuse me," I interrupt. I interrupt their CEO, who, after watching the massacre in grim satisfaction from the sidelines, finally steps into the fray to deliver the knock-out punch. So he thinks, and he growls at me. I don't growl back, but I bare my teeth. We are adversaries—primates, not civilized humans—the mood is primal, and I am not soft or deferent. I stand up. And I move to the head of the table where their pile of "we're going to make you do this" papers is stacked, ready for our surrendered signature.

And I start to, calmly, methodically, rip them up.

As I rip, I start to talk.

I-fucking-love-it.
—Hurts.
And-you-fucking-love-it.
—Yes.

I am… angry. I am angry because they were unethical, really. Because they fought like Brian. Because Brian is unethical. Because I'm married to him. I'm angry, because they didn't play fair, and because they almost destroyed my big chance (I am selfish). I am angry, and my anger fuels me. I am brilliant. And I am right. I argue law, and the law is right, and it is so clear, so obvious, that there is not enough money in the world to convince any judge-lobbyist-legislator that I'm not.

I have them over a barrel in ten minutes.

"Our client," I say, "did not want to do things this way. Our client, against our advice, came here with this ridiculously generous agreement…" I walk away from their, now shredded, papers, to ours, "because he is a gentleman. He did not think the publicity resulting from this kind of litigation would benefit anyone." I pause. I let them think that while it does not benefit us, it doesn't particularly hurt us… but it fucks them over, thoroughly.

That moment of psychological warfare I learned from Brian.

"But given your opening position, as I see it now," I say, "You sign this, now… or we go back to Calgary and start filing the prepped paperwork for… what shall we call this? End-game?"

I win. I don't need a mediator, arbitrator. The silence is my applause.

My senior partner and the client are on their feet. The client touches my shoulder. His hand slides up my neck into my hair, and then down my back. He would embrace me and take me on that boardroom table right then, and I know it. I look at him, but don't smile.

"How much time are you willing to give them to sign?" I ask instead. "Five minutes?"

"I think we should give them ten," he says. "Ten minutes to think it over?" he asks the CEO. Who is white. Red.

"Get that cunt out of my boardroom," the CEO says. The words come out ragged. "We will discuss it when she leaves."

"No," my client says. "You will discuss it with her."

"No," I say. Pull out my phone. Set the timer, the way I do it for Alexandra when I give her a five-minute warning. "There is nothing to discuss. Five minutes."

The documents are signed in 3.47 minutes. We are in the elevator in 4.10. In the lobby of our hotel in 20 minutes. At the hotel bar in 23.

That's when my sexist-racist mentor speaks, for the first time since I started talking in the board room.

"Fuck. Little girl. Fuck," he says. "Fuck, fuck, fuck. Fuck! I wish I could say it was I who taught you how to think like that. Fuck."

Thank you, Brian.

And... I don't love him in that moment. No. But I am so grateful.

The client orders martinis. I excuse myself. Text Brian, "We won. Can I talk to Alexandra?" Spend a few minutes listening to sweetness and joy, anchor myself in her reality. Stop at the bar, and give the bartender instructions that my drinks are to look like martinis but contain water. He gives me an odd look. I touch my throat as if to finger an absent necklace, look at him with a "I don't want to have to tell you this" feeling, and, while he may not understand, he nods. Will comply.

An hour later, my senior partner exits. "Don't get my girl too drunk," he tells the client. "She's got more thinking to do tomorrow." My career, I know, is made. I'm going to be partner next year. My client knows this too...

I so love that he's your client...

...and as the old man leaves the bar, his hand slides down my leg.

"Fuck," he says. "That was... incredible. Incredible." And, made bold by three martinis, "I would have taken you on that boardroom table. With all of them watching. Fuck. It was incredible. Thank you."

"I know," I say. I don't touch his hand. But I let my thighs move apart a little. He responds.

"Another drink?" he asks. I shrug. "Or..." is he bold enough for this? Yes. "Or... we could just go upstairs."

"We could," I agree.

We do.

And?

—Aaah... and?

You know what I want. Deliver.

—I can't. I can't. It's... he's a little drunk and high on achievement. And it's my achievement, really, but as the night progresses, it becomes "ours." And I resent that. But I'm already naked and committed. And he, although starting to share the credit, is still grateful and worshipping me, and so...

You endure?

—I participate.

Clinical.

—No. I... fuck, how do I put this into words? I try to find the restlessness that drove me to chase this file,

71

this trip. I try to find the anger that fuelled me in the boardroom. That's what finally does it, what throws the switch for me: I keep on reliving that moment. Ripping up those papers. Saying, "Five minutes?"

Hearing "Get that cunt out of my boardroom…"

—Even that. I think he's reliving it too, really. We're fucking each other, but our minds, thoughts are in that boardroom… I don't remember what the sex was like. I don't remember what he did. What my body felt, did.

But you were thinking "Get that cunt out of my boardroom" as you came.

—You can think that if it pleases you.

It does. And then?

BLACKMAIL

THEN WE FUCK IT up, as people who have "occasion" sex almost always do. It wasn't about us. It was about that win, and we should have just let it be what it was. But we don't. When he comes to Calgary, I go back to his hotel room after meetings, after dinner…

This hotel, my slutty lover?
—Sometimes.

And when I go to Houston, he assumes my bed is where he's heading to after our conferences. And it's all right, I guess: it doesn't interfere with my life in a material way. It makes me feel… I know Brian's probably fucking around and it doesn't matter, because so am I. But I'm not invested, exposed.

Except, of course, for the fact that I'm fucking a client and I'm a young female partner in a profession full of misogynist pricks who would rip me into shreds if they knew…

And that's why it ends, I think. It would peter out anyway—there is insufficient passion and attraction there. Not just on my side: it's not about me, for him, at all.

You are an occasionally available cunt and any other willing woman would do.
—I'm fungible. Exactly.

It would peter out anyway, but one day, in Houston, he's sloppy. Puts a hand on my leg during a meeting. In front of colleagues. And that night, when he comes, it's while he's whispering into my ear, "I wish they knew I was fucking you."

He becomes a career liability. What do you do?

When I go back home, I transfer all his files to another—male—partner. I tell him the relationship is making me uncomfortable. I say, "It's nothing I can put my finger on—I'm in no way accusing him of doing anything inappropriate. Not at all. I'm just... not comfortable."

To my mentor, I'm more blunt if not entirely honest. "He wanted a mistress not a lawyer," I tell him, when he demands what the fuck. And I add, ass-kisser, "You taught me better than that." The story goes around the firm, quickly. I'm commended, informally, by our managing partner for doing the right thing for the firm. A few months later, the new lead partner tells me that after a few drinks, the client refers to me as "that wanton slut? You wouldn't believe how much she liked to fuck." And apologizes for not standing up for me. Important client. Important file.

If I were innocent, I suppose I would be outraged. As is, I shake my head and say, "I knew my instinct to pass on those files was right." And, sycophantically, I add, "Thank you—for taking it. And for... well. You know. I realize the client is always right. I don't need you to defend me. But I'm glad you didn't believe him."

My beautiful hypocrite.
—It's a double-standard world, still. Were I honest, my career would be over. His, unaffected.

This is probably the point at which I make the decision, conscious or not, to never fuck another client. Or lawyer. The decision to stay away from academics and pseudo-intellectuals was made some time ago.

My next lover is my first artist.

And I am so glad you started that pattern. Fucking artists is an excellent hobby. Although knowing I'm part of a collection also makes me feel cheap and ubiquitous. An interesting feeling.
—I think you are my first successful artist.
Am I? And how does my Elizabeth define success?
—You're paying for this hotel room.
You are my first cynical lover. I like it. For the next leg of the story, I want you on all fours...

MAGIC CARPET RIDE

HE'S NOT A very good artist, of course. Nor, to be perfectly honest... well, what he is, really, is an amateur photographer who works in his father's rug store. Heir apparent to an established, staid business. With a twinge of rebellion in his soul. Which he channels into the camera— and taking nude pictures of his lovers on his father's precious Persian carpets.

Oh, yes. Now that's a photograph I want to see.
—I might have kept a few... if you still remember the next time you see me, remind me. I'll look. They weren't really very good.
You don't sound very enamoured.
—I wasn't. He was... there. And not for very long. I'm almost surprised I remember him.
Why did you fuck him then?
—I was in a mood.

It's, really, Brian's fault: he asks me to pick up my own birthday present...

A carpet? Fuck, Brian. Losing game, man.

"Forgive me, love—I was going to surprise you, Annie was going to get it and it was going to be there in the house for you when you came home, but she can't now, Zia asked her to come stay with Sasha," he tells me, and I pretend to be understanding, because, Sasha, responsibility. But I drive to the carpet store after work seething with anger. The boy's sweet, helpful. Big, liquid eyes. Helps me carry the carpet to the car, makes some kind of light—but satisfyingly disparaging—comment about how my husband should be doing this work. Brushes against me and I don't pull back. We stay too close as we load the rug into the car, and he doesn't create space when we're done. Neither do I.

When I hand him my business card, it might as well have "Call me when you want to fuck" scribbled on it. He calls me three or four days later. Asks me if I would be interested in posing—he has this idea for a photo series—beautiful woman, beautiful carpets.

I'm naked 20 minutes after entering the store. We're fucking a dozen poses later.

On the carpets?
—Yes. I get terrible rug burn. Brian notices it, says nothing.

I come back... I don't know, three, four more times. Not every time he calls. I don't want to...

You don't want him to think you really want him.
—Perhaps. I don't dig deep into my motivation.

The last time I see him, he asks, bluntly, for oral sex. It's funny—until he asks, I don't even realize we haven't. He hasn't gone down on me, nor I on him. Our sessions follow a very typical pattern: I show up. He takes photos. He climbs on top of me. We fuck. He comes. I usually don't. I leave…

You say yes to his request, of course.

He asks me while still photographing me and holding the camera, so I slide off the rugs to his feet…

Fuck, yes…

…and start to fumble with his belt and zipper. His underwear gets caught on his zipper as I pull it down, and the star-spangled banner that covers his tenting cock becomes an immediate turn-off. Who wears a flag as underwear? An American flag to boot?

Would it have been better had it been Canadian, my patriotic lover?
—No, I suppose not. But at that particular moment in time, its American-ness is particularly offensive.

"Here, let me," he says, and pushes my hands and head away to fiddle with the fabric and zipper. And that's when I'm done.

By the time his cock is freed and out, I'm standing up and at the door. I leave without a word. I don't respond to his calls and emails. After two or three days, I block his number.

That becomes typical of the way I conduct my affairs. I don't so much begin them and end them as I pass through them, on my way to the exit as I step onto each threshold.

And each threshold is delicious, enthralling?
—For a little while.

And how does it end?
—Suddenly, always suddenly, I would say painfully, except I think you would call me a hypocrite. But its suddenness does cause me pain, shock. I am in someone's arms, slick, naked, ready... and then I am gone. Done.
—I exit, leaving behind panties, stockings, sometimes unimportant jewelry.
Nasty, nasty bitch.

But I don't fuck around that often. There's the bad photographer. A beautifully tattooed opera singer in Ottawa. An Egyptian poet whose voice I fall in love with, and who recites poetry to me, and sometimes passages from the Qu'ran, in Arabic while we fuck.

Every once in a while it's someone I meet at a conference, or on one of the unavoidable trips to Houston. So I always travel with condoms.

And... relax into me, lover... lube?
—Yes.

CONDOMS IN A SUITCASE

SASHA'S 13 OR 14 WHEN this happens: I'm heading out of town on a business trip—my first piece of a class action, in Montréal, and…

Are you going to see… what was his name? Pierre-André?
—Did you miss the part about how bad the revenge sex was? No.

…and I know I've pre-packed my suitcase and left it on the bed, but when, after showering Alexandra with guilt-ridden kisses, I go into the bedroom to get it, it's gone.

Did someone—the nanny?—take it downstairs for me?
No.
Kitchen? I rip through the house. Finally, knock on Sasha's door—it's during one of the frequent periods she's effectively living with us, even though we're still paying Zia outrageous child support.
"Sasha? Have you by any chance seen my suitcase?"
She opens the door and blocks it. Stares at me.
"You cheating whore," she says. "You foul, foul cheating whore."
Zia's words, in Sasha's mouth.
I look over her shoulder and there, on her bed, is my suitcase. Opened. Disarrayed.

"You cheating whore," she says again.

I am feeling things I cannot allow myself to feel and I close my eyes and make them go away.

"Please put my things back in and give me my suitcase," I say. "I need to leave. Now."

Silence.

She stands there, shaking, hating me.

"Sasha," I say. Court room voice. "Now."

I make no threat, no attempt to move past her into the room. I rarely come into her room; never when she is not there.

I know this is partly because I want to give her the privacy I never had. But also, because what I don't know, I can't do anything about.

She turns around. Throws my things into the suitcase. Among them, lacey things. No sensible night gown. Condoms. A bottle of lube.

I knew it. I love how you travel prepared. Are your lovers ever disappointed, by the way? They think it was all a spontaneous seduction, all their idea, and there you are, fully equipped?

—I don't know. I don't care. I never ask.

"You cheating whore," she says one more time to me as she thrusts the suitcase at me through the doorway.

I grab it and run out. The cab is waiting outside. I slide in, suitcase on my lap. "Airport," I say as I shut the door.

I wonder if I should text Brian.

What would I say?

"Sasha went through my suitcase. Found condoms. Is upset. You should talk to her."

And what would he tell her?

Would he tell her... "Elizabeth and I... we have an arrangement?"

Ha.

I text Annie. "Sasha was very upset when I left." Leave the rest to her; don't care what Sasha tells, doesn't tell her. Catch my flight, spend the time in the air focused on not thinking, not feeling.

Do the case.

Fuck a stranger.

I know I take him up to my room that night at least in part to spite my stepdaughter. Maybe that's why the sex is so bad. But then, sex with strangers... it's just never particularly fulfilling, is it? Its only redeeming feature is its novelty. I wonder if the quality of his orgasm is at all different from what it would be if he had masturbated to one of the cheesy not-quite-porn adult movies hotel room TVs still provide? I feel I am engaged in indifferent masturbation, as soon as my mind wakes up and starts observing my body. Going through the motions. Mechanics.

When there is no desire, there is only endurance.

That thought utterly kills the mood.

So does the suddenly invasive image of Zia. Of Sasha.

Standing behind them, Brian.

Indeed. Although, I think I've told you, there was a rather prolonged period in my life when I thought adultery was hot. I'm not sure it's entirely over.

—That's because you're a psychopath.

I'm an artist with mildly sociopathic tendencies and a lack of comfort with dominant social mores. But enough about me. This is your story.

I don't come. I don't let him stay to cuddle—he wants to. I think about calling Brian—but I won't. And it's too late to call Alexandra—to use her as a pretext to hear his voice.

And so, alone in the hotel room, smelling of sex but unfulfilled, I don't talk to anyone.

I realize that if I had a therapist, he'd pathologize that, me.

Enough third-grade pseudo-analysis, which, in any event, is my job, not yours. What I want to know next—I am so very curious to see how you, and these other women, deal with the emergence of a sexual rival.

—What the fuck?

Well—there you are. You, my lover, I know first-hand, are a woman driven, defined by your sexual desires. My favourite type of whore and slut—don't frown, they're compliments, you're delicious, come here... Zia, you pussy-foot around her sexuality, but she was Brian's wife and I know Brian's taste in women. She must be fucking hot. And I know she ends up with that boy toy kneeling at her feet at Christmas, and probably in her bed before that, no? So yeah, delectable cougar—look how I'm carefully not calling you a cougar, lover, ouch, don't fucking claw at me, or I'll make you regret it....

—I already regret telling you...

Hush, let me finish. I don't know much about Annie yet—because, fuck, the issues you have with this woman are phenomenal—but I do know she sends dirty pictures of herself to a lover. Three women in their sexual prime. Maybe terrified of getting old? Zia for sure—a woman like that—single and over 50? Terrified. How do you react to the blooming, emerging sexual potential in this young woman who is, really, the daughter of all three of you?

—Jesus.

Never mind. Don't think about that too hard. Just tell me this: as your stepdaughter hits her teens, what brings her parents most often to Brian's study for Sasha conferences? What does Zia scream about the most, what's wrong with Sasha the most?

—Sex.

Sex. Case closed... but you may continue to submit evidence, for my amusement.

COMING OUT

SEX. ADOLESCENT SEXUALITY. Fuck. What a mess. Sasha's sexuality springs out at us dramatically and unexpectedly when she's 15. I'm ashamed that I don't really notice it creeping up—I leave it to her mother and Annie, I suppose. They must get her bras and deodorant and introduce her to razors or an epilator—although I suspect Annie might include a lecture about how natural can be beautiful...

There was hair on that mound of Venus, as I recall...
—Could you perhaps not bring that up?
You know I will... Shall we shave off the rest of yours, now, while you talk? I think we shall...

I don't notice that the child is a woman until the child aggressively declares she's a woman by letting her mother find her in bed with a classmate, female, of course, just to up the stakes a little, and an imaginative assortment of toys... which Zia dumps on the desk in Brian's study, screaming, sobbing, ranting.

I make out, "She's not a lesbian! She's just sleeping with that girl to make me angry!" in between the wails. Brian stares at the dildo and vibrator and... "What are those?" he picks up Exhibit "F" with the tips of his fingers. "I'm not sure," I say. I want to add, "Shall we ask Sasha?" but I don't, I swallow the words and look at Brian with something akin to compassion. He is definitely not relishing the moment. He's not wanting to think of his daughter as a sexual being—but what parent does? It's hard…

You admit it, then?
—Yes. Especially for a father, with a daughter? Fuck, yes.
Easier for you, you claim?
—She is not mine. So I have no claim.
Oh, Elizabeth. You're either deluded, or a liar. Don't fucking claw, I said. Go on.

Annie seems to be doing better, she's a little flushed, but she keeps on making, "But don't you remember, we were all young once," noises. Me, I have just one thought: Sasha, Sasha, why did you not lock the door, turn on some loud music before getting naked and noisy with your girlfriend?

Because she wanted to be busted, discovered.
—Yes.

And there she is, slumped in one of Brian's chairs, listening to her mother lose her fucking mind, again. Is she inured? Does it still hurt? Annie rubs her shoulders every once in a while. I'm leaning against the door frame, on the sidelines. I watch Zia in almost mild amusement, and I promise myself, I will not interfere, this is not important. I still remember Zia shouting, "How dare you? How dare you? I love her. I love her and she's mine!" when, after Sasha suddenly drops 20 pounds in the first weeks of junior high school, I take control and stage an eating disorder intervention… and put her in therapy… and… cross a boundary that I had erected for myself when I entered her life…

But you had to. To protect her.
—Don't pretend to understand. And don't fucking interrupt me again.
You know I will. But rage if you must.
—Don't.
Apologies. Please. Go on.

So I don't say a word as Zia screams and Brian and Annie caress. I don't laugh when Annie says, "Bisexual, probably," in an attempt to placate Zia, and Brian counters with, "Pansexual, I think the term the kids use these days is pansexual," college professor up on the young people's lingo, ha. I don't point out that, hey, they could ask her— she's sitting right there—she'd tell them what she wants to identify as. I don't protest or argue when Zia announces that "that whore" (this time, she doesn't mean me, she means the lover, whose name is Jean) will "never, ever cross the threshold" of her house. I don't even say anything when she closes the "conference" by telling Sasha that so long as she lives under her roof, she's not going to "act like a lezzie slut."

Ouch.
—Yeah. She's not subtle…

But when Sasha shows up at our door the next day with two suitcases and a backpack, I make sure her father's house is her sanctuary. Her room ready. With a new lock on the door.

Hell hath no fury like a controlling mother out-maneuvered. Another family "conference."

"Your father is not going to let you act like a slut in his house either!" Zia, screaming.

Mumbling from Brian.

"My father has no right to tell me who I can or cannot sleep with!" Sasha. Screaming. "And neither do you!"

"Annie! Can you please tell…" Everyone, all at once. Looking at Annie. Can you please fix this? Annie helpless, looking from Zia to Brian. To Sasha. Then to me.

Me: "Sasha, could you please go up to your room? Your father will come see you later." Sasha, about to say something—probably, "You have no right at all to tell me what to do!"—rethinking it. Leaving.

Zia: "My daughter!"

Me: "You have no right to make rules in *my* house."

…which sends her screaming, "This used to be my house, you fucking whore," and ensures that nothing is resolved and also that Brian is not at all inclined to do what she asked: neither send Sasha home, nor ban her girlfriend from the house.

You are a manipulative, manipulative bitch.
—No. Well. Maybe. You see… Sasha can't ever lose the right to be in her father's house. Or the ability to be the person she needs to be in her father's house. Do you understand? That it's *my* house, that's fucking irrelevant, I say that to piss off Zia—fine. Manipulative. Yes, I am. This is Sasha's house. A place where she can be safe. No matter what.

I meet Jean the next week. I'm pretending to cook—really just getting in the new nanny's way, and hanging out with Alexandra in the kitchen—when I hear noise and laughter in the entrance way.

"Shush," from Sasha.

A choice: pretend I do not hear them. Or... the other.

"Sasha? Is that you?"

They come in, bashful. Sasha pulling the other girl by the wrist.

"This is Jean," she says. "Jean. This is Elizabeth."

She doesn't say the slut who married my father but I feel it. I contort my face into a smile.

Jean is Sasha's age, size, shape. A mirror of Brian's daughter; even their clothes match. Flushed, embarrassed, she does not want to meet me any more than I want to meet her. I never learn anything more about her, not even how she and Sasha met. I assume they are in school together, but I don't know.

I don't ask.

But. I do this:

"I think we're eating at seven," I say. "Will you be staying for dinner, Jean?"

"No, she'll leave before Dad gets home," Sasha says quickly. The implication, obvious: "Don't tell him she was here."

I sigh. I will not be Zia, but neither will I be the woman who teaches a child to lie to her father.

"Too bad," I say. "He would have liked to meet her."

Pause. Sasha's eyes boring straight into me, the eye contact rare—painful. Incredulous.

"Well, 'liked' is probably not the right word," I correct myself. "He *ought* to meet her."

Jean stays for dinner. She says nothing, eats less. Sasha says nothing. Brian says nothing. I talk with Alexandra and the nanny about their day at the Science Centre.

We never see Jean again. Hear from Annie that the great love affair lasts five weeks, ends in tears and heartbreak.

They always do. And... five weeks is an eternity at 15.

—It can be an eternity at **40** too.

If five weeks is an eternity, what must you think of 50? Are you getting bored, my novelty-seeking lover?

—No. Not yet.

SLAP. Not a nice answer. So no novelty reward for you. But I bet the stepdaughter's shock tactics don't end here.

—No.

PRETTY BOY

A HANDFUL OF girls follow, each introduced to the family with fanfare as Sasha's first true love. I can't remember when Zia finally capitulates and asks Sasha to move back home. I do remember I'm not consulted or told; one day, Sasha's just not there, and Brian tells me Zia came to pick up her stuff during the day, and we're back to our regular "every second weekend at Daddy's" schedule.

I feel…

You feel… what?
—Hurt. Unreasonably hurt.
Reasonably. Don't you think?
—No. A child should want to be with her mother, and a mother should want to be with her child.

And then comes Chuck. Fuck. Chuck: 25 when Sasha is not yet 16. Yakuza-style tattoos all down his back, legs, and arms—which Sasha insists he show us the first time she brings him over—and she brings him over, just as she does all the girls since Jean, formally, awkwardly but openly, reveling in Brian's discomfort, wanting to arouse mine.

She fails?
—She fails.

91

I'm relentlessly supportive. Chiefly as a reactive, neutralizing technique. But also, because I don't love her, I don't care so much. I don't own her. I have no right to control her. No expectations.

Zia's words, in your mouth.
—What?
You heard me.
—Also, I'm a bitch and I love denying her the shock value.
That, I believe.

When she asks Chuck to show us his ink, I say, "Please, please do, we'd all love to see it." And he does as she requests, flushed and embarrassed. And I relax. There's the required leather jacket and motorbike, the earrings, nose-ring, and nipple rings—glimpsed as the shirt comes off and the back is presented—and the concern that he is a decade older than my ardently jailbait stepdaughter.

But he does as she asks him to. It embarrasses him, but he does it anyway to please her.

I know he's all right, she'll be all right.

The bared back embarrasses Brian, of course. The age difference doesn't faze him. I don't realize until sometime later that Chuck's maleness makes up for almost every other defect.

He is too old, too tattooed, too weird. But he has a penis. Brian's daughter is no longer a lesbian. Score.

Zia, who apparently learns little from the Jean episode, flips, forbids him the house *and* her daughter, and calls Brian a negligent father for not doing the same.

"She's going to see him anyway," I try to explain, crossing that line again.

"You'll understand one day," Zia says, tone ominous. She glares at Alexandra, then five. "You'll understand."

Christ, I hope I won't.

Sasha doesn't exactly move in, but she uses her father's house as a love pad. I forbid the smoking of pot in her bedroom.

"Porch, roof, and only when Alexandra is not around," I say.

She doesn't challenge me.

Of course not.

Chuck is, except for those tattoos, Chuck is perfectly ordinary. Fucking boring, really. When I learn that his incredible body art is a perfect replica of Takeshi Kitano's back in the movie *Kikujiro*, I'm not surprised.

The relationship lasts almost six months, which does surprise me: I expect Sasha to get wise to him, bored of his conventional rebellion sooner. The first one or two months are a honeymoon period, that I get. He's her first male lover. Sufficiently older that he is considerate, sensual. So she tells Annie, and so Annie tells me, thrilled to have been told this intimate tidbit by her goddaughter—thrilled that I don't know.

"I think they're really, really in love," Annie trills. I roll my eyes.

So I make Sasha end it…

You do not. I don't believe it.
—I might as well. I fucking know what I'm doing and why.
What? You hit on your stepdaughter's boyfriend?

*—Fuck, no. She's 16, and she hates me—that's
probably just the sort of thing she'd expect me to do,
delight in seeing me do. No, what I do is much more...
Manipulative?*
—Yes.
So. What do you do?

I give Chuck a long, intense look as he leaves the house
one day. And say this:

"He's such a pretty boy. Reminds me of your father, in a
way. Especially his posture—the set of his shoulders." A
pause. "And his hands. For some reason... his hands."

Sasha: "What makes you fucking think I want to hear
that?" But she hears it. Perhaps flinches the next time she
looks, closely, at his hands. It was going to end any way, I
tell myself—but it ends two weeks after I say *that*.

I never tell Annie; Sasha doesn't either.

Fascinating.
—Why?
You're guilty, and ashamed.
—A little.
*And you don't understand your motivation at all. I love it.
Shall I give you absolution?*
—No.

94

PROMISCUOUS POLYAMORY

MORE BOYFRIENDS. MORE girlfriends. The first piercing, another, another. Tattoos. Various acts of self-actualization, rebellion, identity-seeking. Most of them centred on sex.

But of course. What else is there?

The last major one is when she's 18 or 19, legally an adult, and running out of things to do to shock her parents.

So fucking cynical.
—Well. We're at two dozen piercings, several arrests, an attempt to work as a stripper, and two drug-related visits to the ER at this point. She crams a lot into her teens.

It's the addition of "polyamorous" to her "gender-queer, pansexual, not bisexual, but I'd rather you called me gay than bi or straight if you have to label me" identity. Annie loves it. I remember her cooing: "It's so beautiful. Many loves."

And what did her uptight stepmother say? To the declaration of polyamory—which, incidentally, I will mock mercilessly if you give me a chance, although I know you won't...

—I said, that it was smart. That it was ridiculous to get all tied up in one person at her age.

Ah. Of course. You would say that.

The polyamory family pow-wow is the first one we have at which I laugh, out loud, uncontrollably. "They all know about everything?" Brian says, perplexed, and I can't help it, I laugh until tears come out of my eyes. I remember, sharply, his excitement at fucking me in Zia's bed—hiding in the shadows of door archways—the sneaking around in the university halls. I can hear—"But what's the point? Where's the excitement?"—as clearly as if he had said it. He stares at me, confounded. I laugh more. Infuriate, of course, Zia, who is already screaming that it's unavoidable, with the type of man Brian is as a father, and the type of example she has at his home—dagger eyes at me—*unavoidable* that Sasha would turn into a slut, slut, slut...

That's when I stop laughing, leave the room, slam the door...

Sasha's waiting in the hallway.

"Does she really think there's something she can do, any of you can do to make me be something I'm not?" she demands of me. Braver with me than she would dare be with Zia.

"Probably not," I say. Pause. "If you need a ride to the STI clinic, by the way, ask me. I'll take you."

Is she impressed?
—No.

"Why? Because you also think I'm a disease-ridden slut?" she screams.

96

"No. Because you're smart and if you're going to have sex with multiple partners who have sex with multiple partners, you're going to test yourself regularly and make sure your partners do the same," I say.

I still remember, my voice. Suddenly, exhausted. And the look in her eyes before she says, "Is that what you do, Elizabeth?"

And what do you say?
—"Yes." I just say "Yes." What else is there to say?
And do you drive her to the STI clinic?
—Every six months.
Unshockable, unflappable Elizabeth.
—I'm not unshockable. But who am I to… judge her?
Right. The foul cheating slut-whore who married her father. Who travels with condoms and lube in her suitcase, and who fucks artists as a hobby.
—You…
For the last fucking time—don't claw. And don't slap. That's my job. Is Zia's boy toy—what was his name, Stefan? —is he an artist, by the way? He has that fucking pretentious look about him. I recognize an aspiring member of my tribe. Oh. Do you take him away from the ex-wife, spite Zia again? Let's get to him. I want to meet the boy toy. Now.
—He is an artist. And he's coming. Be patient.
You know I'm not. I hope the rabid ex-wife introduces him to you. Flaunts him. Snaps his leash. And you, angry, pounce…
—Um, no, that's not quite what happens. Although— there is leash snapping, of a sort. And *his* wife is there.
Wonderful. I can't wait to meet her, too.

EDUCATING PHILISTINES

BRIAN ALWAYS BRINGS me flowers when he starts falling for someone new. I wonder if he notices the correlation? If he knows he does that? Or if it's all subconscious guilt, oozing out in the most conventional, obvious gesture?

When the flowers stop coming, the affair has become complacent. She probably gets none either. Were I looking for evidence, the way Zia did, this would be the point at which I'd start finding turquoise threads in the dryer lint trap.

When he starts to get bored with his Other, he starts to miss me. Texts me when I'm at work. Hangs out in the dining room while I work after dinner.

Brings me coffee up to bed on Sundays.

Then comes a plea that we do something together. "A real date, Liz? It's been much too long." I usually oblige. Why not? We dress up. Go for dinner. Theatre. Concert. He seduces me through the evening and when we get home, he exerts himself fully and my body benefits.

So clinical.
—I don't love him. Should I pretend?
You don't love him. But you still enjoy fucking him.

—Yes. We've established that he's good in bed. And most strangers aren't.

It's on one of our "real dates" that I meet Stefan.

It's the opening of a new exhibit at the Esker Foundation Art Gallery in Inglewood. His choice of that particular venue surprises me. "I want to do something new," he says by way of explanation. "I feel stuck in a rut. You know? Let's do something different." I wonder if his last conquest told him he was boring. Made him feel old…

Women are so cruel.
—Girls are even worse.

The gallery's full of people who think they're important, and so inevitably includes a few of my colleagues. Clients. Competitors. Someone introduces me to someone who introduces me to someone who introduces me to Stefan's wife. Stefan's wife—who's got a touch of Zia around the mouth and eyes—is standing beside a god.

I wait for her to introduce us. But she does not.

"Elizabeth," I introduce myself and reach out a hand. "Lawyer. Philistine. Woefully out of place here."

"Stefan," he takes it. Smiles. Beams. His smile pours into me, fills crevices I had no idea were empty. "Artist."

"House-husband," his wife corrects. Hisses. "A stay-at-home dad." Pauses. Her mouth, tight already, tightens more. "Isn't it great, the freedom men have these days, to pursue non-traditional roles." Her intent is so nakedly to wound, to hurt, I take a step back. But Stefan is unperturbed. Smiles at me again.

"One of my favourite hobbies is educating Philistines," he says. "Here. Let me tell you why, if someone asks you what your favourite work from the exhibition is, you should tell them that it's this piece." He gently, unobtrusively takes my elbow and rotates me towards a gaudy canvas.

"That's horrid," I say. He laughs.

"Only at first glance," he says. His wife steps in-between us. Again says something meant to hurt. He looks at her, smiles.

"You're right, of course, my love," he says.

I watch Stefan interact with his wife and I want to laugh. He is soft, yielding, agreeable, tranquil. But is he? He gives up no point. He artfully refuses to rise to any of her barbed baits. And he uses each exchange as an opportunity to send me a look. The look is first cautious and careful, connective. "Do you see how she is? Do you see how I respond? Do you see how I'm misunderstood?" And he picks up on my dislike, my visceral reaction to her, and the more comfortable, confident in his reading of me he is, the bolder his looks are.

"See what I have to put up with?" one of his later looks says. "Yes, I know you know I fuck around—yes, I know you know I want to fuck around with you. But don't you think it's totally justified?"

"Totally." The third time I hear her speak to him, I decide I'm going to fuck him just to spite the nasty bitch.

Is this not Zia's boy toy you're introducing me to?
—Well. Not yet. Not exactly...
Oh, Elizabeth. You little whore. Come here, let me reward you in advance for the nasty thing you're going to do...

He gives me the opening right in front of her.

"I'd love to show you my work, sometime, if you're interested," he says. We exchange phones, punch in each other's numbers as she watches. He will show me his studio. "A tack onto the garage," she snorts.

"My sanctuary," he says.

"I can't wait to see it," I say.

Does she know he is picking you up? Or that you are picking him up?

—I don't know. She is so angry and bitter and snappy… I'm not sure what she sees.

And where is the husband with whom you are supposed to be on a date?

—Ah. That's rather amusing. As we walk into the gallery, he turns white. Wants to leave. I follow his eyes, and see a tuxedo-clad caterer staring daggers at him. "Someone you know?" I ask. "Someone I do not want to see," he says.

He leaves?

—He leaves. I stay.

And acquire a new lover. Well done, my lover. Fast-forward to your studio visit. I want you naked and fucking.

FUCKING ARTISTS

STEFAN FOLLOWS THE three day rule before he texts me. "Is today a good day to continue a Philistine's education?" It's not. But the next one is. I don't wish to make him wait.

Or yourself?
—I suppose. The scene in the art gallery, the reminder that my husband fucks around. Yes. Defensive adultery. Again. And also—he has the face and the body of a god. I am eager.

Absent the need to diffuse or ignore his wife's barbs, in the citadel that is his studio, Stefan is more real. More vulnerable.

"I'm not…" he says, "I'm really just an obsessed amateur. If everything you see reminds you of something else… well, there's a reason for that." He's embarrassed, suddenly shy. "The word, I suppose, is derivative," he says. Pulls out a canvas.

"This is from when I was obsessed with Degas," he says, as he shows me ballet dancers.

"This is from when I was pretending to be Dali." Watches, melting landscapes.

"Did you have a Picasso period?" I ask, sitting down on a paint-splattered arm chair.

He laughs. But is he hurt?

"No," he says. "I would not dare attempt to imitate the master."

Talent is a peculiar thing, I think, as I look around his studio. Is he talented or talentless? Does it matter? The space is beautiful. The overall aesthetic effect created by the easels, the displayed, stacked, half-finished and abandoned canvases, the bookshelf filled with jars of paint brushes, egg carton palettes, and shiny unopened paint tubes affects me.

"It's beautiful," I tell him as soon as I enter. I please him. He smiles. Encircles my waist. "It makes me so happy," he says. And I'm not sure if he means—that he's happy I think so, or if the space makes him happy.

Both, perhaps.

We both know my looking at his paintings is foreplay. So one of the thoughts I have, as he shows me canvas after canvas, is, "Where?" The chair in which I sit down is comfortable... but small...

Stefan stands behind me.

"There's paint on the chair," he says. "You'll get your beautiful clothes stained."

"Clothes can be washed," I reply, without turning my head. "Dry cleaned."

I wait. I expect his seduction of me to be... smooth, practiced. Our first encounter, the hook up effected in front of the wife, suggests he's done this sort of thing before, and often. But he stands, still, behind me. Watching me wait? I turn my head to look at him. Smile. He bends down. Meets my lips. Fully. Parts them with his tongue, and his teeth pull on my lower lip. Then the upper.

"I should like to paint you," he says, my lips still between his teeth. "I should like to paint you in various states of *déshabillé*."

My suit jacket comes off. Buttons undone.

Groan. I approve not his technique. And I approve not my Elizabeth succumbing to it. Disappointed.

—I did not succumb. I came there to fuck him. At least in part to spite his wife, because I was in a mood.

Excuses, excuses. And I'm not at all getting turned on by this story. Look at my poor limp cock. Try harder.

—I'm not sure I can. My experience of Stefan—then—is coloured by my experience of Stefan since. I can't quite... he was very, very beautiful of course. That didn't go away. But my desire for him was so fleeting...

Yes. You apparently pass him onto your husband's first wife. Fast-forward to that part.

—I can't. That doesn't happen for weeks. First he is my lover... and to understand what happens later, you need to understand...

I need to be amused. So tell the story like you care. You wanted him. Remember that, tell me that.

—I'll try.

Buttons undone. "Oh, yes." "Such a fiddly zipper. They should be outlawed. Ridiculous things. And oh, more buttons? My muse. You did not dress for me at all!" I rub against him, hold onto him. Inhale his scent of paint. And, what? Wood-smoke, cinnamon. Pepper?

My trousers off, onto the floor. And delight. "Now that's better. Beautiful..." I'm wearing fuck-me panties, and he plays with them, pulling them here and there, fingers and hands around them, but never in them. I respond, immediately. Wet and wetter, rubbing more eagerly, chasing his hands and fingers with my throbbing clit, swollen lips.

Finally...

"May I?" he whispers into my neck as he slides them off. I moan in anticipation. He stops them at my knees. Pulls away. Steps away.

"Yesss," he exhales. "Now. Hold that pose."

I am in the chair, naked from the waist down, shirt on but unbuttoned. Hair disheveled. Breathing hard. One leg stretched straight, long in front of me, the other bent, tossed over the arm of the chair.

Panties stretched between my knees.

So aroused.

He starts to sketch.

I get wetter.

"Don't move," he says, as one of my hands travels to my cunt. I moan.

"You can moan, but don't toss your head back. Stay still... stay still..."

It is torture. It is the most arousing thing I have ever experienced. I stay still. I suffer. I want.

When he finishes sketching—it could be five minutes or 50, I have no idea, it feels like an eternity and yet not long enough—I almost come as soon as I feel his breath on my neck. And I do come as soon as his thumb grazes my clit, almost before his fingers thrust inside.

The fucking that follows once his clothes come off and he bends me over the armchair—he takes me from behind, looking, I know, at the sketch of me on the easel, and not at the me in front of him—is anti-climactic.

The anticipation is everything.

It so often is.
—Yes.

I am anticipating getting to know your sister-in-law. Intimately. Don't disappoint me.

—I'm very much afraid I will.

You're not afraid. You hope you'll disappoint me. You're looking to fill the… how does that hackneyed quasi-legal phrase go? The letter of the agreement, but not the spirit. You're not so much setting the scene as evading the main issue. But, lover, the more you talk, the more you betray. You know, better than anyone, that safety lies only in silence.

—What about metaphor?

Metaphor always betrays. But by all means, try it.

—All right.

GUILT IN A TEA CUP

THE FIRST LICK of green tea ice cream is one of the most wondrous, sensual pleasures in the world; the first sip of hot green tea can be the promise of a meal. But the last sip of tepid green tea, from the dregs of an empty pot, is almost chewy. It leaves a bad aftertaste. And yet, you still drink it.

I don't.
—I still drink it.

I'm drinking it sitting opposite Annie. The tattooed barrista at Café Artigiano, who has served me dark roasts with room for cream for six months, is staring at me as though I've never been in a coffee shop before as I struggle with the list of choices. "Green tea café latte?" he suggests, finally. I curl my lip in disdain. "Ugh."

"Well, this is what we have," he says. Exasperated. "Coffee in all its permutations. Black tea. Green tea. Decaf versions of all that. Assorted juices and waters. Pellegrino?"

And all the while he's thinking—why don't you just order coffee the way you do every other day?

"Because I choose to make myself suffer!" I want to shout at him.

Instead: "Just a green tea, then. Thanks."

He offers me choices. I offer him a look of hate. Silently, he rings through my purchase, gives me a pot of hot water with a smattering of leaves in it.

"Green tea?" Annie says. "Green tea? You don't usually drink green tea."

Of course. Annie knows what I drink—when I'm with her—better than I do. When Brian and I visit her and Brian's brother, which is both rarely and too often, she pours me a cup of scalding hot, stinky tea. "Earl Grey," she says. "Your favourite. Isn't the smell of bergamot just incredible?"

"Earl Grey," I repeat. Is that what I drink when I'm with her? I don't notice. I don't like it. I don't like tea. I don't know what bergamot is.

"Thank you," I remember to say. But ungratefully and without real appreciation for the gesture, because—well, what I really drink is coffee.

But I don't drink it with her. I only drink it with people I love.

I'm flattered.
—Shut up.

"I wanted to talk to you about Sasha," Annie says. I nod. I know this. I also know she knows the only way to get me to meet her is to make the topic of the meeting Sasha. When she says, "Let's catch up!" I'm too busy. When she says, "There's a new restaurant I want to try," I say, "I hope you enjoy it." (When she, explicitly, texts, "Come with me!" I counter with "I'm on a cleanse.") When she outright asks me to do something with her, I just say no.

I realize… she hasn't done that in a long time. Not since the book club fiasco—and that was for Sasha, anyway. How long ago was that? A year, maybe more. No other overtures since then, bar that mis-texted photo. Perhaps, she's learned.

Stupidly, the thought makes me sad.

You know what makes me sad? That while pretending you're telling me about your sister-in-law, you're going to be talking about your goddamn stepdaughter again. Tell me you at least bring up those mis-texted pink panties with her.
—Of course I don't.
Does she?
—No. We don't talk about anything else, ever. We only talk about Sasha.

Once, she says, "I'd like to talk to you about Alexandra," and I snap, "You never get to talk to me about Alexandra."
But Sasha. I will talk to her about Sasha.
Because Sasha talks to her.
Because Annie loves her.
Because I feel such guilt.

I love you wracked with guilt. Guilty women are easier to control.
—Fuck off.
That's the game you and I are playing. Do you not know that? I am looking for the key. And you're trying not to give it to me. But you want to play, and so you keep on talking, and so eventually, you will.
—I won't.
We'll see.

Talking about Sasha, these days, always, mostly involves Annie strategizing how to present to Zia whatever new thing Sasha's done or wants to do. Annie has, possibly, already tried to talk her out of it, and failed. She has now talked herself into a place of unconditional support for the latest piercing, tattoo, boyfriend, girlfriend, life plan. How are we going to make Zia support this?

We're not.

It doesn't matter what it is.

She'll freak. Rant.

Come into my house (which used to be her house—she'll remind me of this immediately, relentlessly) and disrupt supper. Better yet, at night and wake up Brian, me, scare Alexandra. At some point, make it clear that Sasha's sexual proclivities—eyebrow piercing—desire to go on a WOOFing trip to Europe—volunteer in the Sudan—are all the fruit of her dysfunctional family experience, Brian and Zia's divorce, and so, my fault in their entirety.

I will, at some point, leave the study, and lock myself in the bedroom. I won't open the door to Brian when he finally gets her to leave and comes upstairs. When I find him sleeping on the couch in the morning, I won't feel compassion, only resentment. And so it goes.

And Sasha will still be pierced, tattooed, gay, thinking about dropping out of school, taking welding instead of a BComm, dating a stripper ("Don't call her a stripper! She's a sex worker!" "Right…").

I've never dated a stripper. Or a sex worker of any kind, actually, my whore fantasies notwithstanding. Hmm. I like your stepdaughter, you know.
—Don't fucking go there.
I'm not. I like… I like what she does with her angst. It's healthier than what you do with yours. But then, she has help. You're helping her direct it.
—What? I am not.

So fucking unaware. Or a liar. In either case, I love it. Come here, and pretend you're unaware of my hand, spreading you like this…

—Not while I'm talking about Sasha.

Ah. I suppose not. All these parenting minefields I'm not aware of. Then lie face down so you don't see me. And I will take a page from Brian's book and give the mother of his children a massage.

—I am not…

You are. Keep on telling the story, and you'll find out.

I stare into my cup of tepid green tea—wish it were coffee—and try to listen to Annie. Sasha. Couple. Dating. Serious, so serious. Not, Annie says, an occasional *ménage à trois*—her French accent is atrocious—but she's *dating* them both, actually, she is moving in with them… and they're into BDSM, the language they use—he's Sir and she's Kitten and Sasha's their Pet…

I tune out, until she says, "What should we do?"

"Nothing," I reply, promptly. This, at least, I know.

"I don't mean…" Annie flutters her hands. "I don't mean about *it*. I know—I mean, I know it's odd. And she's 20, and yes, that's very young to be moving in with someone, and dating a couple and all that is a little odd, yeah, but she seems so very in love…" And she talks on, circling around her lack of comfort with the nature of the couple's kink—but also, I realize, a little excited about it all, which is fucking weird and awkward and I don't want to hear it, and so I interrupt her.

"She's almost 20. She'll do whatever she wants." My chorus for the past two years, the past decade…

"Of course, of course," Annie agrees quickly. Fully on Sasha's side. Anxious to show she knows more than I do, is more connected to the situation, to Sasha, than I can possibly be. "She met them in May, when she started working maintenance at the Stampede Grounds. You remember?"

I remember. The source of another parental conference-shouting-match from hell. Zia convinced Sasha was taking the janitorial job purely to spite her... and possibly right about it, at that.

"I know they haven't known each other very long, but Sasha has such good judgement," Annie says, and I snort tea up and out my nose. Cough.

"I'm sure they're nice people," I tell Annie. And actually, as I clear the tea from my sinuses, I decide that it's probably true. For all her rebellion, Sasha has been quite particular about her people. They've been, of course, pierced, tattooed, frequently unemployed, occasionally—but not that often—stoned, but nice. Jean, Chuck, all the in-betweens and the ones who followed.

Weird. But good eggs. At least: harmless.

"You know, I was a little bit concerned, at first," Annie says, and I'm surprised. She is usually Sasha's unconditional advocate, no questions asked, no critical judgement used. If such judgement exist, there is never an admission made, to me, that Sasha's choice, path could be wrong, dangerous—even questionable. "What sort of people date as a couple? Or call their lovers pets? It's... you know... um, it's..." She's flushed.

I'm amused.

"People have all sorts of kinks," I say.

They do, my lover. Tell me about some of yours.
—Do you not prefer just discovering them as you go?
Mmmm, sometimes. Sometimes, I like revelations. And you know I like to be shocked. Would you enjoy having another

woman in bed with us? Tied, perhaps to that chair,
watching? Waiting?
—Not particularly. My exhibitionism is very particular,
and I am not a voyeur. And my sexuality is not
particularly fluid.
In other words, you like boys.
—I like men.
Then I'm so glad I am one.

The rest of our conversation follows a well-trod path. We
remind and reassure each other—or rather, Annie reminds
and reassures me, and I nod—that what's important is
Sasha's safety and security. That we need to keep her talking
to us (to Annie; we both know she doesn't talk to me). No
matter what. Bla bla bla, shoot me now, because what that
all means is another fucking conference around the study
table, at which Annie will be supportive and loving, Brian
helpless and ineffectual, and me... present, unnecessary,
resented. We—Brian and Annie, mostly Annie—will
attempt to coach Zia into acceptance. Fail. Annie will listen
to Sasha rant against her mother. I will listen to Zia rant
about how I ruined her life and am ruining her daughter's.

Everything will be my fault.

My current meeting with Annie is as pointless as the future
parental conference about Sasha's planned living arrangement
will be. The tea in my cup is cold and disgusting.

I drink it and grimace.

Telling. I told you metaphors betray as much, more than,
straight out confessions. What happens next?
—The entirely expected.

LABELS

AND... HERE WE go again. Room. Lamp. Arm chairs. The same fucking conversation. Or, rather, attempt at conversation deteriorating into a monologue and then screaming.

For reasons that confound me, Annie chooses to tell Zia *how* Sasha met her couple—whom Zia hasn't met yet, of course, whom Zia hadn't heard about until Annie told her about the planned co-habitation—whom Zia has already forbidden Sasha to ever see again. "What are you going to do?" Sasha jeers. "Throw me out of the house? Wait, you've already done that!" and she walks out. Slams the study door.

Zia barely pauses for breath. She hyper-focuses on the fact that they met at the summer job Annie, Brian, and I encouraged Sasha to accept against Zia's express will.

I don't even remember what it was that Zia had found offensive about the job—actually, I lie, her daughter, doing menial labour, maintenance, janitorial work? Everything about it would be offensive to Zia. I do remember her screaming at Sasha that if she weren't "so pierced-tattooed-shaved and freaky looking," maybe she'd be able to get a proper job...

"Fuck. You." Sasha yells back at her mother at *that* screaming session. I silently applaud. About time. Careful not to look at Sasha, though, careful not to connect.

"His name is Tim," Annie is saying at *this* screaming session. Zia is starting to vibrate. By the time Annie gets to the part where Tim and Sasha are sharing a joint at coffee break—what the fuck is she thinking, telling the story like this?—Zia's shaking.

I wonder if Annie's going to tell the next part—which she had told me over tea—about how Tim shows Sasha his tattoos.

Oh-my-fucking-god. She's not. Is she?

"He noticed her tattoos, asked her who does her ink," Annie tells Zia.

Jesus, what's wrong with her?

Tell me… what she shouldn't tell Zia. And why.

What I know, because Annie has told me… it goes like this, he asks her, "Who does your ink?" and she tells him. All the details. Artist's name. The for-public-disclosure version of the meaning of each tattoo.

"All of mine are hidden," he says. "I'll show you later." Later is the next break. Behind a food truck, in the shadow of a dumpster.

She gave her… I mean, she, Sasha, gave Annie, her godmother, that much detail? And she passed it on to you?
—She did. And she did.
That's a little fucked.
—Yeah…

His pants' belt loosened, his shirt off.
"Touch them," he invites. "I'm not shy."
Tattoos, apparently, are seductive.

I can see that. I do approve of Tim, by the way. I hope he gets copious pussy, and that this seduction ends with Sasha on her knees beside that dumpster, a cock shoved down her throat.

—Shut up.

Oh, I step on another parenting minefield, and the stepmother bristles, again. Forgive me. I go back to my earlier point: is it hard, conceptualizing your daughter— stepdaughter—as a sexual being?

—No, I don't think so. I get that, I see it. I saw it at 15. And now, she is almost 20. She is all sensuality-primal-exploration. I accept that. But...

You are the mother bear and she is the cub. Understood.

—You cannot. I can't tell you more. This is sick.

I withdraw. I apologize. Just the essentials. I won't transgress on this ground again. I promise. Here. I won't even touch you for this part.

—I don't believe you.

Watch me. Or keep your face down in the pillow, as you wish. But talk.

They kiss, touch. There are sparks. And he whispers, "I can't wait to introduce you to my girlfriend."

Her name is Claire or Clarissa or something like that.

And Annie has lost leave of her senses and is apparently going to narrate the whole story exactly the way she received it from Sasha—or at least the way she passed it on to me. And then she's going to talk about pets, kittens, sirs, and bondage. And Zia is going to kill us all as a result.

I interrupt.

"None of that matters, does it," I say. "The point: she's 20. Independent."

"She's doing this just to spite me," Zia says. "Like always. She hates me. She doesn't appreciate..."

And we're off.

"She does all this just to torment me," Zia's chorus. The exact words she used with Jean. With Chuck, during virtually every single Sasha conversation. It's not about Sasha, ever: it's about *Zia*.

She is the centre of her universe. Aren't we all?
—I fucking hate her. I. Hate. Her.
I know.

"But don't you remember, we were all young once," Annie continues to spout clichés. I look at her, confounded. She's manic, jittery. Useless—everything she's saying counter-productive. Is she always like this, and am I seeing her clearly for the first time? Well-intentioned, but totally ineffectual, as ineffectual as Brian. Worse, self-sabotaging, Sasha-sabotaging?

"Disgusting!" Zia. And then, at Brian, "And you don't even care!"

Brian, helpless, useless, fucking useless.

And you?

Me… already exhausted. Barely aware of what it is that we are "discussing." Screaming about. Zia's mouth, open. Words. Annie's mouth, open. Words.

Pointless.

I wonder, yet again, why I have to endure these women, this drama, trauma in my life.

Look at Brian.

Not worth it.

Alexandra's upstairs, in her room, in bed, hopefully watching YouTube videos with headphones on.

Fuck them and this pointless conversation. I'm going to go be with my daughter. As I leave, Zia screams to my retreating back—as she always does—"And your whore of a wife doesn't even care enough about your daughter to stay!"

I shut the door on them without slamming it—my act of self-control seems more offensive, more powerful than an act of wanton anger would.

Sasha's standing in the hallway. I look at her without seeing her. Hate her, at the moment, for being the cause...

Look at me, engage in the blame game as fully as Zia...

Hate myself...

"Did she settle down?" Sasha asks. I shake my head. She sighs. Looks at me. I think... she would apologize if she could. Not for dating a couple, not for planning to move in as a "pet" (and what the fuck is that, exactly) at 20 with people she's just been fucking for a handful of weeks—not for being bisexual, pansexual, polyamorous, gender-queer, whatever label she's identifying with at the moment—I don't mean that. For... unleashing Zia on us. On me. I think... yes, I think she would apologize. I think, in this moment, she is sorry. She, of all people, knows.

"It's all right," I say, as if she had said *that*. I think about saying, "We're used to it," but decide not to. Instead, I ask her if she wants something to eat. She shakes her head. I leave her, go upstairs to see Alexandra, who's fallen asleep with headphones on. Take them off, carefully. Retuck her in. Love her.

That night, when Brian comes to bed, I slide towards him and into him. He's shocked, because I rarely initiate... and never after Zia's been in the house...

You're more likely to lock him out of the bedroom after one of those sessions, you said.
—Yes.

What's different this night?
—I don't know. I don't know.

"What do you want?" he bites an earlobe.

"Violence." My request is simple. "I don't want to think."

But it takes a while before my tape turns off. I'm thinking, not of Zia, but of Sasha. I've managed to push past hate and blame. Not quite the resentment—the resentment is there, powerful. Coupled, I suddenly, I realize, with envy. At her incredible freedom.

Freedom?
—Freedom.

She speaks, plays, and explores polyamory, sexual orientation, the relationship matrix in a way that... Fuck, when I was her age, the label for that behavior was... promiscuous. Easy. Confused. Slutty. And those were the less damaging labels.

Ah. If she had fucked a middle-aged professor with a wife and daughter, she wouldn't have felt she had to marry him.
—I don't think *that.*
You do. That's why you envy her.
—Is it? I don't know, Christ, I don't know. I'm struggling to put it into words, even now. I do know... I envy her... fuck, even just the vocabulary.
Polyamorous, not promiscuous? My conflicted, morally conventional slut. That's amusing. Me, I'm glad I'm too old to have had to go through that mind-numbing navel-gazing and label seeking.
—Are you? What's your label?
None. I just like to fuck. As a white male who loves to fuck women, I speak from a place of privilege, of course.

Speaking of places, I want you at my feet for the next part of the story.

—I can't talk with your cock in my mouth.

Who said anything about my cock in your mouth? None of that until you're done. Get down there. I want your head against my thighs—just so. My hands in your hair. Your hands...

—...on your cock?

No, I'm bored of that. You're distracted by what you're saying and not paying enough attention to me. I'm going to press my—totally flaccid now, by the way, lazy lover—cock against your cheek. You are going to put your hands on your breasts. Cup. Tug. Caress. When you get yourself sufficiently worked up, I might help you out with my foot.

—This is not that kind of story.

Then make it such. Change it to suit my need.

COERCION

THERE IS, AS I predict, no point to the latest battle, just as there was no point to agonizing over Jean or Chuck or any of the interchangeable "unacceptable" lovers who came in-between. Sasha lives with Tim and Claire-Clarissa for three months. All is bliss, Annie reports regularly, just the thing Sasha needs, she's so happy...

I don't notice, until much later, that she *reports* on this to me much more often than necessary. Every couple of days, a text. "Hi, Elizabeth. Just wanted to let you know, heard from Sasha. Everything's great!" "Hi! How are things? Had coffee with Sasha. Madly in love!" "Sasha says hi! So great to see her so much in love! Pays to be open-minded, doesn't it? Everything's great!"

An excuse to connect.
—Yes. But I don't see it, don't notice. All I see is... a reminder of how connected *she* is to Sasha, a reminder of how I'm not. And, "All is great." "All is bliss."

Until it isn't, and, on a Sunday night in late August, the doorbell rings at 11 p.m. Brian's out, entertaining (fucking, I suppose, I don't care) a potential faculty hire. I think he's forgotten his keys, wonder why the fuck he's ringing the doorbell instead of texting me so that he doesn't wake up

Alexandra and the current nanny-house help. I open the door, already resentful.

Sasha. A backpack, two suitcases. Red eyes.

"I'm moving in," she says. "Unless you've turned my room into a boudoir or rented it out or something?"

"It's exactly as you've left it," I stand aside to let her pass. Don't offer to help with the suitcases. Watch her struggle with them up the stairs. Lock the door. Briefly consider shooting the deadbolt, to which I know Brian does not have a key, across it. My resentment, stirred by my expectation of seeing him at the door, hasn't changed targets with Sasha's arrival.

Of course not. She is just another facet of him, in this guise.
—Don't analyze me.
But that's why you're telling me the story. Isn't it?

Annie reacts to this development—the end of the romance, living arrangement, ownership, whatever—by insisting that we must all get together, "All the important, strong women in Sasha's life," to support Sasha, to "show her she is loved." And, we agree, Zia and I...

...because you love Sasha...

...because Annie knows how to manipulate us. And I think Zia wants to gloat, maybe? Unleash a satisfactory "I knew it!" or dozen at us? And me, I don't know, I just don't know how to say no, and maybe...

Maybe?
—I don't know if this is true. Or hindsight. I think, maybe I'm a bit uneasy. Something's off, something's not right.

With Annie? Have you had any other mis-texted dirty pictures from her?
—No. Nothing. And I'm not—you know I'm not... intuitive. Sensitive.
You. Are. So. Sensitive. Especially... right... here...
—Aaawww...
But I'm only doing this if you keep on talking...
—Aaa... I'm... unsettled. That's all.

When I get to Café Blanca, Zia and Annie are already there, talking. Not about Sasha and her broken heart—but about Zia. And her empty one.

Cliché, unworthy of you.
—I'm repeating what was said.
Paraphrase more creatively then.

"All I want," Zia throws her voice dramatically—the way I would in a court room, actually, I pause for a moment and wonder if she learned this trick from Brian or whether he copied it from her—"all I want is someone to stand up for me. You know? Someone to stand beside me, and hold my hand, and tell me, 'You are my world. I will do anything for you.'"

"Zia..." Annie tries to stem the flow. I try to remember the last time Zia had a boyfriend, lover, date. Ever? Surely, at some point... I hate her, but she is beautiful.

Passionate. Voracious, even.
—Don't editorialize either.
She terrifies me, make no mistake. Frankly, I don't think I could handle her. Few men, I suspect, could...

I wonder if I'd know? How I'd know? Only if Annie told me. Would Annie tell me?

"You don't understand!" Zia says dramatically. "You, married to the love of your life for the past 17 years. You have it. You have *it*!"

Annie's face... Jesus. I avert my eyes. Zia sees me but pretends she hasn't. What she says next, she says just for me.

"Someone to grow old with," she says. "You'd think, after the way I have been treated, after the way I have been betrayed, I wouldn't believe in true love, wouldn't you? But I do. Oh, I do."

I roll my eyes. Hoping she sees me—but she doesn't.

"All I've ever wanted," Zia says. "All I've ever wanted! *Love*. A man who lives for me, who wants me, who understands me, who *completes* me..." Eyes full on at me, and, she fires, "I had that, once." She doesn't say, "Until he met you, cheating whore," but we all hear it.

"Hi, Elizabeth," Annie says. Face composed, now. "Sit down. Or will you go get your tea first?"

I think that if I get a cup of tea, I might not-so-accidentally trip and spill it on Zia, so I opt for Pellegrino. Sasha's at the table by the time I come back, sipping from a water bottle she's brought in with her.

So there we are, together again, three crones and a maiden, around a table in a coffee shop.

You know what I just realized? This is going to be another fucking book club meeting vignette. Except maybe without the book.
—Maybe a little.
Fuck. Standing up. Against the wall. ...

I don't want to be here. I want to be—anywhere else. Naked in Stefan's studio. Suited up and in a board room with a lying client. Robed and in a court room. At home, playing at housekeeper and cleaning the kitchen floor, badly.

Anywhere, but here.

Yet here I am.

I root through my purse for my phone, a chocolate, a distraction. Fish out a half-chewed pencil, which might be the remnant of our last cheerful foursome.

Which was the actual book club meeting, with which you began the story?
—Yeah.
You try my patience, woman. This better be good. Or this— no, hands on the wall, don't fucking move them—won't be...

Annie is asking Sasha, earnestly, how she's doing. Sasha's answering in monosyllables and evasions. Zia is holding a compact and examining her carefully made up face with care. Suddenly she snaps it shut; the noise is so loud, Annie stops talking.

"Anyway," Zia says, looking at me. "I have way fewer wrinkles than you."

I'm rolling the pencil in-between my fingers and the desire to stab her in one of her Botoxed eyes is almost irresistible. Sasha laughs, a strangled, half-choked sound. Annie's mouth drops open.

I don't say, "Botox is an amazing thing, innit."

I don't say, "Cunt."

I look back at her, at the beautifully made up face, the outlined eyes, the extended lashes, the mouth so perfectly designed only a drag queen could do it better...

"You look absolutely wonderful for your age," I say. And smile. Kindly.

It's the nastiest, meanest thing I could say, and we both know it.

So does Sasha, whose eyes widen in terror. I glance over and I see—fuck, I did this. Shoulders hunched, tense. Preparing for her volatile mother's explosion, and I caused this, I exposed her, my fault.

"We are an amazingly good looking family," Annie says. An attempt to deflect, but it fails, fails. I don't turn to look at her, my attention split between the tensed up Sasha and the about-to-explode Zia. But I do wonder how someone so empathetic, as sensitive as Annie professes to be… can yet have such a gift for saying, doing the wrong thing. All the time.

Because we are not a family. We are not related, not in a real way, not in a way that means anything.

What binds an ex-wife, the second wife, and the sister-in-law of both?

Nothing permanent. Nothing that matters.

Sasha speaks. "I only hope I am as beautiful and young looking as you when I'm in my fifties, Mom."

Conciliatory. Loving.

Zia preens, for a moment. Then, what? Notices the reference to her age. She is 53. At least. And she bristles.

"You can hope," she says. Jesus. "But I doubt those piercings and tattoos will age well."

Jesus.

Jesus, god I don't believe in, never, ever let me hurt my daughter this way.

Annie is speaking, panicked, babbling, random. About what? I can't hear her words and I don't believe she's really aware of what she's saying: it's as if she believes, if she talks enough, she will drown out, erase, what is really happening. I can't take it anymore.

I get up.

"I'm going home," I say. I look at Annie. There are terrible things I want to say to Zia. I can't. But I can hurt Annie. And so, I do.

"We are not a family," I say.

I could add, "I'm sorry," "Forgive me," but I'm not, and she won't.

As I start walking away from the table, I hear a sob, and then, Zia, "What are you crying about? There are long-term consequences to the things you do when you're young! And if you choose to punch holes in your face…"

I let this happen all the time. I am silent and on the sidelines, because I am afraid to intervene, because I don't think it's my place. Because I am guilty. Because I hate Zia and I don't love Sasha.

I turn around.

"Sasha? Do you need a ride home?"

She gets up without a word. Not that it would be heard; Zia is now storming, making a scene; Annie's remonstrating, trying to calm her down.

Everyone in the café is looking, listening—or worse, pretending not to.

We won't be able to come back to this coffee shop. Ever.

I let Sasha come up to me, then pass me before I start moving again. I am bringing up the rear. I realize I'm protecting Sasha from attack from behind, and that pleases me, although it might be too little too late…

The fact that I have that emotion and thought shames me and by the time we get to the car, I am awkward, angry.

So ashamed.

Of what, why, I don't know.

All the usual things. More than 15 years of wrong decisions, choked down impulses. Attempts, all so bad, of making work what shouldn't have been in the first place.

Sasha bursts into tears as soon as we are in the car, doors closed.

"I hate her, I hate her, I hate her!" she screams, and she is 15, ten, five again, not a young woman of 20. "I fucking hate her! How can she say such things to me? I. Hate. Her!"

What can I say?

"I'm so sorry." Meaningless. Why bother. But I say it anyway. How do you live with, love a woman who loves you so much—I know she loves Sasha, I know—but who kills you, destroys you with every word?

I don't know. I left...

—Don't you fucking probe, I didn't mean to say that. *Silent as a castrated mime. Fucking curious. But silent...*

Sasha stares at me. Hates me too. "She's mentally ill," she hisses. "Fucking psychopathically crazy."

"I'm so sorry," I say, again.

She looks at me again, and it hurts. Then she speaks, voice harsh.

"I don't think it's all your fault."

That's the closest, I think, that I will ever get to absolution.

And then, immediately, her tears dry up. The sobs stop. She will not, she should not say such things about her mother to me—I know she is thinking this, I know she now feels shame. Guilt. Consciousness of betrayal.

Fucking life.

I say nothing. Drive home.

When Alexandra is asleep, I text Stefan. "Any chance?" "In my studio. Come from the back." This time, there is no sketching, no foreplay. I strip naked as I walk through the door, and then stand against it. "Fuck me as if you wanted to destroy me," I demand. "Whatever you want." He complies. Or tries to.

It doesn't work when you have to ask for it.
—No. But he doesn't know how to perform otherwise.
Such a pity. Is your favourite thing about me that I don't need to be given instructions?
—Would you take them if I gave them to you?
No.
—That's my favourite thing about you.

UNGRATEFUL

ANNIE TEXTS ME that night, a fucking essay of a text that's unworthy of the writer she claims to be.

She explains to you in detail how and why you are a family? —No. She doesn't even allude to that. She just doesn't want me to think *she* thinks I'm a cheating whore...

"Elizabeth, I just want you to know," she keeps on repeating, "that I understand. I understand completely. I know it's easy for others to call it cheating, to throw stones, to condemn you. But I know it's more complicated than that. I know two people who are meant to be together cannot be confined by the laws of conventional morality..."

It makes me gag, and I don't read through most of it.

But you get the subtext? —Not exactly...

I am dim, and I don't put together the dots for months, although, in retrospect, I see that Annie litters my path with clues ever since the incident of that photo. But I do know exactly when things click for me and I realize that she's planning to leave Brian's brother. It's when she brings Alexandra the ribbon dress.

Alexandra and Brian are out at her choir practice—say what you will about my adulterous, selfish, self-absorbed husband, he performs chauffeuring duties extremely well. My cynical self might whisper that it gives him the opportunity to more freely text with the paramour of the moment. But I know that's not really true. He likes feeling he's doing something useful. And he likes the one-on-one time with Alexandra in the car… I think. I rarely try to get inside his head. Maybe I should do that more.

But I don't care enough to.

Fuck. What's wrong with me?

Anyway. Brian and Alexandra are out, and I'm at the dining room table, parsing lies, and pondering whether I should get a hobby other than fucking artists. Am I bent over this work because it really needs to be done, or because, alone in this house right now, I have nothing else to do? I fight the urge to text Stefan. I have this awful thought that perhaps I am lonely, so fucking lonely, and that's why… and I don't want to follow that thought, so it is with relief that I see Annie's text.

"I have something I want to drop off. Secret for A! Are they still at choir, and are you home?"

"Yes. Come by."

She knows that I am home alone before she texts. She knows our schedule almost better than I do. She's offered to drive Alexandra to choir if Brian and I cannot—I refuse, always, although Brian will, when I am out of town, take her up on that.

"Why can't she just have her own fucking baby?" I yell one day, at Brian, after Annie's offer to do something with the newborn Alexandra, to give me "respite," a word I fucking hate. "Why does she want mine?"

"Liz! Be kind!" Brian's admonition to me.

"Don't. Fucking. Call. Me. That!"

Sleep deprivation makes one irrational. Rude.

I know I'm possessive of Alexandra. I love her ferociously and humbly. I am never tempted to sing my own praises as a mother—I have no confidence that I'm doing anything right. I am insecure and so possessive. From the beginning, I need her to be mine, and I need Zia and Annie to keep their hands off her. Zia's not interested but Annie... Annie oohs-and-coos over Alexandra when she is newborn and seems to know just how to hold her—I don't. I have to learn and it's hard and I'm awkward and every time I start to think I've got it, I look at Sasha, her scowl, her anger, her pain, and I'm reminded what a fuck up, fraud I am.

A possessive fraud.

I change nannies every six months, because I don't want Alexandra to get attached to them—them to her. I don't call them by their names, even. They're all "Nanny," interchangeable. I know it's fucked. I know I'm irrational in the extent of this desire—and I know where it comes from. I don't need a therapist to tell me any of this.

I know I should probably do something about it.

But I don't want to. And I keep Annie away.

She keeps on trying. Through ten years of rebuffs, she keeps on trying.

The doorbell rings in time to keep me from asking, again, that confounding, "why"—*why* does she keep on trying? — and there she is, walking through the door with a large HBC bag.

"Elizabeth," she says, by way of greeting. I have trained her not to hug or kiss me, although I do let her hug and kiss Alexandra when they meet; I am aware my crazy possessiveness is... well, crazy. We walk past the dining room table strewn with my papers. Into the living room. Annie perches on the ottoman.

"I made something for Alexandra," she says. "For her birthday? Or maybe Christmas? It was going to be a graduation present..." she pauses, and she glows with pride, and suddenly, I almost love her, because I know that glow of pride is not for herself, not for what she made, but for Alexandra, for my brilliant daughter, who will be graduating from grade six at age ten, and I glow with pride too.

"It was going to be a graduation present," Annie continues. "But I finished it early... and I can't wait... I wanted to show you, now. You can give it to her now. Or Christmas? Birthday? As you think best. I just wanted... I wanted to show you. And to explain..." her voices trails off. She plunges her hands into the bag—it has a nautical theme, and its pattern of sailboats, fish, whales, and tridents gives me something to look at, focus on instead of on her face.

She pulls the ribbon dress out of the bag.

It is amazing. A wearable rainbow, a work of art. I am mesmerized. Annie gabbles, nervous, about the tradition of ribbon dresses among the Mi'kmaq, how she learned about it from one of her writing students, how she thought Alexandra would love it...

"She will," I say. "It's beautiful. Thank you."

"I wanted to show you, right away," Annie says. "And explain." Eyes down to her lap again. Then, in my direction, but not at me. Over my shoulder. I turn my head to follow her gaze. It's fixed on the vase of half-dead bamboo that she gave to me and Brian for some occasion. Last Christmas? Maybe an anniversary...

"I know you don't like it when I get you, or Alexandra, presents," she gets out finally. "But this is different. Special."

"It's beautiful," I say.

Awkward silence.

I realize Annie's afraid to give Alexandra the ribbon dress. And it's my fault, of course. I am resentful. Ungracious. I accept the gifts, when I must, with a scowl.

Annie accepts the scowl… and keeps on showing up at our door, in our lives, an offering clutched in her arms. One day—a hideous stuffed seal. Orange, with blue stripes.

"For Alexandra's orange collection," she says, thrusting it into my hands. I sigh. Am so clearly—always—so ungrateful. All of Alexandra's stuffed animals are either orange or turtles—in two cases, orange turtles. Almost all of this menagerie come from Annie, who once heard Alexandra declare, "I love all things orange! And, turtles!" and proceeded to attempt to buy her love with… all things orange.

And turtles.

I am too cynical. It is thoughtfulness. Maybe.

But I really, really love Alexandra and I never buy her a single orange teddy bear.

I bet you bring her a gift of some sort every time you go to Houston or Montréal. Books about turtles, for example.
—How do you… Maybe. And I do keep the house stocked with oranges and orange paint and crayons. Ha.

Point: Annie can do no right thing by me when it comes to Alexandra. What I really want is for her not to love and connect with my daughter at all. She already has my stepdaughter.

But I expect that if she did that, I would resent her as a cold-hearted bitch, who doesn't care about my real child while lavishing all her love on my false one.

Oh, Christ, do I think of Sasha as my fake child?

I do not think of her as mine at all.

She is Brian's and Zia's. And she sometimes lives in my house. Which isn't my house at all, but hers. And Brian's. And, 15 years ago, Zia's.

In this house, 15 years later, I am still the interloper.

I am the interloper, and Annie belongs. In this house. In Zia's life, Brian's, Sasha's.

Is that why I fight so hard to keep her away from Alexandra?

"I want to explain," Annie says again.

I am fingering the ribbon dress and thinking about the orange stuffies, all the gifts. Invitations to Disney movies. Dropped off baking. For Alexandra, for Alexandra. Why? Why does she want to connect with *my* daughter so much?

And it occurs to me, for the first time, that maybe all of these gifts are attempts to connect, not so much with Alexandra, but with me.

That Alexandra will love the rainbows and colours of the ribbon dress—but I'm the one who's supposed to understand and appreciate how much work it took.

And all I do is tell Annie to fuck off. Even in the way I say thank you.

"Thank you," I say again. And try very hard to mean it.

Annie rocks on the ottoman. Doesn't meet my eyes. Has she heard me?

"You are all very important to me," she says. "Family—family is very important to me. Sasha. Alexandra. You and Brian." She doesn't say Zia, but of course. Zia.

I know this. Annie is what makes us a family. She's the glue. The only reason we ever do anything together. Know anything about each other.

She is the reason Zia is still allowed in this house. ("For Sasha," she counsels me, over the years, and I do manage to listen. "For Sasha.") Without her…

"I don't want to lose you," she says.

"What?"

"I don't want to lose you," she says.

And that's when I know. She's leaving. She's leaving Brian's brother.

But she wants to keep his family. Including me.

Why?

Fascinating. And does she get to?
—What?
Does she get to? Does she get to keep you?
—That is the question, isn't it?

This is the first time that I get... the first time that I realize—maybe not fully, but at least get an inkling of—that if Annie wants to keep Sasha, she has to keep Zia. If she wants to keep Alexandra, she has to keep me. And vice versa. That we're all connected and interdependent and messy, and it's a very uncomfortable thought and I don't like it.

You have some fascinating processing flaws.
—What?
Never mind. We'll explore your fear of being human later. Right now, I want to hear more about your avowed lack of gratitude...and your sister-in-law's relationships with your daughters.
—Daughter and stepdaughter.
Your daughter and your stepdaughter. Your daughters. Note my emphasis. And don't protest. I'm hearing things you don't realize you're saying.

DUPLICATE

ANNIE IS SASHA'S godmother, a role it is hard to say who takes more seriously: the nominally Islamic Zia or the ardently un-Christian, nominally neo-Pagan Annie. Sasha's unchristening takes place when she's two or three, and Annie's newly married to Brian's brother. The pictures that Annie takes out every year on the anniversary of the event show a bunch of barefoot people in the backyard of our house—Brian and Zia's house then, Sasha's house—and Zia, in traditional Islamic dress. Or, at least, a head scarf (designer, expensive). Long-sleeved dress (long, flesh-hiding, but definitely not modest).

If Annie and I had a different type of relationship, I'd probably make some type of remark at the outfit. Something sneering. And Annie would say, "You know Zia. She always has to dress for the occasion."

But we don't, so I don't, and she doesn't.

The godmother gifts the goddaughter with a necklace, at best quaint, at worst hideous—a mishmash of glass, plastic, and metal beads, from which dangles a large, shining red heart. From a distance, especially when light hits it in just the right way, it's spectacular. Beautiful. Up close—well, I said it. Hideous.

Whenever I see it on Sasha's neck—when I enter her life, she wears it often and always on the anniversary of the christening, her birthdays, Christmas—it makes me think how its blend of kitsch and taste is such a perfect reflection of Annie. Or what I know of her anyway—what I choose to know of her.

Sasha loves the necklace—the amulet. That's what she calls it, always, her amulet. And Annie loves that Sasha loves it.

So I suppose it's inevitable that Annie fucks it all up by getting its duplicate for Alexandra.

She doesn't do it right after Alexandra's born. Instead, she circles for months around the idea of some type of unchristening for Alexandra.

As her campaign unfolds, I see, first-hand, how the atheist Brian and born-Muslim-and-occasionally-aware-of-it Zia ended up with a pseudo-Pagan, Catholic-influenced "baptism" of their daughter. Annie's campaign is soft… but relentless.

You like using those two words to describe her.
—They fit.

Fortunately, I am not soft.

"I think Annie really wants another goddaughter," Brian says one day.

"Life is full of disappointments," I snap.

Annie brings the amulet over on a Sunday afternoon, when I am napping with a six-month-old Alexandra. Brian, in his study marking papers or exchanging dirty emails with a grad student, fails as gatekeeper.

My door creaks open slowly. "Sorry," Annie's voice. The fog of a sleep-deprived mother, in me. The anger at being woken up. The exhaustion that makes a rational response impossible. Another event in which Annie violates my boundaries, crosses lines she doesn't see I've drawn.

"I'm sleeping," I hiss. "Alexandra's sleeping." I realize, years later, that Annie, childless Annie, doesn't get the enormity of her sin. How fucking wrong it is to wake up the mother of an infant.

"I won't be but a minute," she says. "I just couldn't wait. I finally found it. Look! Look!"

She sits on the bed beside me, pulls a box out of her purse.

"Look!"

I look but I don't see. My fingers fumble with the box. I want to throw it at her. Instead, I get the top off. Sparkle of light. Red. And.

Amulet.

Glass and plastic beads. The heart.

I pull it through my fingers.

"For Alexandra," Annie says. Unnecessarily. "Just like her sister's."

That is the first time that I realize... Alexandra and Sasha... will be... *are* sisters.

I am a terrible stepmother.

I let the necklace drop onto the bedspread. The bedspread is old and lumpy—Alexandra has puked over the "real" one—and the red heart on its hideous chain of beads disappears between the lumps.

"Thanks," I say. Then fall back onto the pillows. Close my eyes. Fall asleep—no faking necessary—almost too quickly to hear Annie leave the room, sobbing.

Sasha is wearing her amulet when she sees the duplicate, still on the bed, on the bedspread—at sleeping Alexandra's feet, I think. She tiptoes into the bedroom, perhaps to peek at her baby sister. Perhaps to take something of mine from the closet. She sees nothing but the *second* amulet.

And she feels... everything. Every betrayal. And she rips hers off her neck and throws it onto the floor. Stomps her feet and screams.

Screams and screams.

Wakes up Alexandra.

She's gone when, livid with anger, I reach the bedroom. The door's open. Sasha's necklace, chain broken, on the carpet, beads everywhere.

My intention to yell at my stepdaughter disappears. My anger at Annie, also. I pick up, first, Alexandra, and then the broken necklace. Then, fish the brand-new one from the folds of the bedspread.

Put both of them into the box Alexandra's came in. And the box into my bedside table drawer.

I realize you're setting up something profound. Fine. But now I need to be put in the mood to fuck and tales of your motherly devotion are not doing it for me. Switch gears. Tell me you put the box in... oh, your sex toy drawer, for example.

—I did. Incidentally, unintentionally. There is no meaning in it.

There doesn't have to be. But there is meaning in the necklaces. And the ribbon dress. Which you accept ungraciously.

—Yes.

SECRETS IN A VELVET BAG

ANNIE LEAVES *WITH* the ribbon dress. We decide to save it for a Christmas present for Alexandra—too long to wait until her birthday and graduation, and Annie thinks I'd disapprove of a "just because" gift, and well, maybe she's right. As she's heading out the door, her phone pings—a personalized whoosh that sounds like a combination of Irene Adler's notifier on Sherlock Holmes' phone in the BBC series and a frustrated cat—and I watch Annie exert all her will power to not check her message that second. I don't have to watch her go down to her car to know that the phone will be in her hand as soon as she thinks I cannot see her, and that she will respond to the text before she drives away.

And then check to see if she heard back at every red light.

Some experience with this type of behaviour, lover-mine?
—A little.
Is that what you do when I text you?
—Not anymore. But perhaps I did once. All of my new loves excite me.
Cold. Hearted. Bitch. Except you're not. But please, continue to pretend you are... while I show you you're not...
—Aaah...

Keep on talking…

So as Annie dances down the walkway away from my house, I know that she has a lover and that she is planning to leave Brian's brother. This knowledge changes the way I feel, think about Annie. I don't think it does—I don't realize it does until much later—but it does. Immediately.

She becomes real to you. A fellow adulteress.
—No! I never think of myself as an adulteress, not really. Nor of her as one. But maybe, a fellow…
Human?
—Fuck. What do you think I thought she was before?
I don't know. I do know this—don't pout, lover, come here, let me kiss it all better before I cause you pain again—you do not like thinking she—anyone—is at all like you. You are alone, an island, a unique snowflake. But now you see yourself in her. Or her in you. Something like that.
—I fucking hate your analysis. And it's not true. I see myself reflected in Zia all the time: at least, I see her as what I could be, what I…
Bullshit. You watch her, obsessively, to make sure you do not become her. You revel in not being like her. But we're talking about you and Annie here, not you and Zia. Here, I'll give you something you will accept. When you think of Annie with a lover… you see her as a fellow sexual creature. Experiencing an emotion you understand. You don't understand why she wants to love you. Why she loves Zia. Frankly, you don't quite understand why she loves Sasha—or your daughter. But you understand why she'd want to fuck a man other than her husband.
—Asshole.
Prophets are never appreciated.

I know it's because I'm thinking of Annie in a different light that I find myself in her house a few days later. My presence there is the result of me saying yes to several requests I'd usually, invariably, say no to. First, "Elizabeth, any chance you can give me a ride home after work? Car's in the shop and I'm stranded downtown! I can wait until you're done for the day." I make her wait until 7:30 p.m., because it's Alexandra's choir night and I won't see my daughter until she and Brian get back from practice later in the evening.

But I say yes; I could have said no—three months, three weeks ago, I would have said no.

And, when we pull up to her house, and Annie says, "Come in, please come in, I have something I really want to show you," I agree, and come in, and not just because it's 7:50, and Brian and Alexandra won't be home for another hour.

You're curious.
—Perhaps.
And guilty.
—Guilty?
Guilty. So-guilty. Meditate on that while you continue the story, and I continue this type of stroking...

We're passing through the living room when her phone pings, with *that* ping. I see a glimpse of her face as she looks at it, and avert my eyes—her joy is naked, obscene. And for the first time since I've known her, I'm hit by her vitality, her beauty. Passion.

You see a woman who likes to fuck.
—Yes.

And it shocks me because I've never thought of her as…
fuck, I've barely thought of her.

I try to imagine Brian's brother as a lover passionate enough to match what I see she is in that moment. And I can't. This, the achievement of Brian's mother—a law professor who can't keep his cock in his pants, an accountant who doesn't know how to take his out.

Don't make assumptions.
—Who are you defending here, exactly? Brian or his brother?
Oh, Brian's brother, the invisible, elusive Brian's brother. Whose name I've stopped you from giving me, but I think it might be necessary to slap one on him now. What shall we call him, lover-mine?
—His name is Julian.
Julian? I don't like it. Insufficiently ordinary. Still. I bet you he has hidden depths.
—Why? And if you say men know these things about men, I'm fucking going to leave.
Fuck no. Men know nothing about men. If we're lucky, we learn a few things about women—at least the types of women we like to fuck. But thanks to you—or despite you, in a way—I am learning about Annie. And so I've a pretty good idea of the type of man she'd want. He'll have hidden depths. I promise you that.
—Like you?
Ha. Me? I'm utterly shallow. Don't you know that yet?

She sees me looking and then looking away, but her eyes and attention are all for her screen. I see it—for a moment, she forgets I am there, the only thing that matters is on that phone.

But I am there. And she remembers.

"Just go wait in the bedroom, I'll be right there," she says as she pushes me into the hallway, then across the threshold to her bedroom. I feel awkward. Intrusive.

I would never invite her into mine. Who does that? Why does she want to see me in here, not in the living room, like normal people?

She doesn't. She's going to take half-naked selfies for her lover on her couch, that's what he asked for, I fucking know it, and she doesn't want you to see, so she wants you safely stowed somewhere with a door.
—Now who's making assumptions?
You're making the same one.

I sit on the carefully made up bed, corners as tight and repressed as when Brian makes our bed.

I look around.

I don't snoop. Never. I know Sasha keeps—smokes—pot in her room, maybe other things, but I don't go in there unless she invites me. I would not look in her dresser drawers, under her bed or behind her pillows for anything. Does she know this? Perhaps. She's gone through phases when she's left her journals and sketchbooks lying around the house. On couches, coffee tables, the floor. This happens: "She wants you to read them!" Zia says, reaching for one. "No!" I tear it away from her. "No. If she wants me, you, to read them, she will ask."

There is that awful exception, that poem we find on her sixteenth birthday, laying on the kitchen table.

"It comes like this—first, a tickle on the outside of her consciousness, a scraping, scratching, a sense of discomfort and then—a sense of disquiet, growing, swelling, alarm rising, disorientation—and then, a pause in breath, a tightness in the chest, and fear—and then, here it comes,

145

bigger, faster, louder, scarier, until it crashes over her, batters her, drowns her, and she can't breathe, swim, move live—she is lost, she is destroyed, she is gone."

Annie, stupid, stupid Annie, writing teacher Annie, as she reads it, exclaims, "Beautiful!" And I stare at her, think, "Idiot, idiot," and make arrangements to put Sasha in therapy, again. Zia and Brian are both appalled. Annie doesn't know whose side to take. "What's best for Sasha?" she asks helplessly. Sasha screams she hates me. Goes to see the therapist religiously for six months. Lives.

I agree with the sister-in-law. It is beautiful.
—It's a metaphor, and it's awful. The wave is Zia's anger, emotional volatility. And it's killing her daughter. *And you know this, why?*
—I have a fucking brain, and I don't romanticize... I just know. Now stop forcing me into digressions: the point, what I'm trying to tell you, is that I don't snoop.

I find out about Brian's first affair through *unintentional* snooping, unsuspecting curiosity. I still remember the moment before my eyes fell on that letter, the pink ink, the almost childlike scrawl, as the last moment of my peace and innocence, in a way. Delusion, I suppose. I don't regret the knowledge. Hell is being a constantly deceived wife like Zia. Purgatory is knowing karma is kicking your ass. I choose purgatory over hell, willingly.

Still.

I don't snoop.

So. Sitting alone in Annie's bedroom, I barely look. I am as uncomfortable in my sister-in-law's most intimate space as I am in my stepdaughter's. Maybe more. I don't belong. I feel an intruder, violator, just by the act of being.

Although, I am vaguely aware that I... that I don't resent the invitation, this time.

I don't like this awareness.

In the middle of the bed is a pink velvet bag. With a white A stitched on it. More—to A from N. I wonder idly who N is, know it's not any of Brian's brother's initials, or is it? I don't know his middle name. Maybe it's Nathan. Nicholas. Naheed.

Ha. Probably not *his* initial. But people get embroidered bags from mothers, sisters, friends.

I realize I don't know if Annie has sisters.

I realize she's probably told me. A dozen, a hundred times.

I don't know.

I don't listen.

I reach for the bag. Caress it. I love the contrast of the sumptuousness, richness of the velvet and the innocent kitsch of the baby pink colour. It reminds me of Alexandra's play-princess dresses and Valentine's Day Barbie. I wonder if it captures an essence of Annie. This N, who got her the bag, does he—she—know the essence of Annie? Does the colour say something about Annie, about N, about their relationship? Or was it the last bag on sale? Or—I can hear Annie saying this, I can hear her voice, "I found it at Value Village and couldn't resist. I love imagining who N is, who A is. I pretend to be A, of course, and N? Who could N be?"

I realize I'm assuming, accepting—I am convinced my sister-in-law is having an affair.

On the evidence of a mis-texted pair of panties, two witnessed phone pings, and that "I don't want to lose you" sentence...

—Yes...

One of the objects in the bag is long and hard and I think of a dildo, and I immediately laugh at the image of Annie with a dildo, and then I chastise myself. Any woman married to Brian's brother deserves to have a good dildo, I think, and it's at that moment that my brain decides to reach into the bag.

And I pull out… a hot pink dildo. A light pink harness. A bottle of Astroglide.

The bottle is in my hands, and the dildo and harness on the bedspread, when Annie walks into the bedroom.

Awkward.
—You'd think…

"Oh, you found it," Annie says. "What do you think? Do you think she'll like it?"

"What?" I ask.

"Sasha," she says. "Do you think she'll like it? I wanted to get her something… you know. Feminine. Not too penis-like."

I'm not sure whether to laugh or cry. So I nod. Put the dildo down. Trace my finger over the stitched A. And then the N.

"I saw the bag at Vintage Closet and couldn't resist," Annie says. "I know it's the wrong initials, but isn't the colour, and the texture, just the thing? You don't think… maybe I should pull out the letters before I give it to Sasha? Anyway. What are you getting her?"

Sasha's birthday. Which I've forgotten. Again.

"An envelope of cash, I suppose," I say. "As usual."

I don't say much else. I leave. I don't think about how Sasha's going to react to this kind of present from her godmother. But I do smile at what Zia's reaction might be if she finds out.

I almost laugh, actually.

What do you get your stepdaughter for her twentieth birthday, by the way?
—A trip to fucking Peru to do the Inca Trail and see Machu Pichu. Almost as expensive as the Red Cross-sponsored-but-you-pay-for-it volunteering trip to the Sudan she wanted to do for her eighteenth birthday.
Generous to a fault.
—No. With Peru, I thought getting her away from her... from her family for a bit would be the best present I could get her.
After that coffee shop fiasco. The mother's meltdown, yes?
—Yes. And with Sudan, there was a level of... well, the usual triggers. Zia screeching, "She's going to fuck everything that moves and come home with AIDS!" And Sasha screaming, "How dumb do you think I am?" And Annie, wringing her hands and talking about safety, and "Oh, love, how brave of you, how wonderful, that's just the sort of thing I would have loved to do when I was younger." And Brian silent, and then, "How much is this going to cost?" without looking at me and Sasha. "Dad, fuck, why is it always about money with you?" And me. Just buying the ticket, making the decision, to make it all stop. And then taking Sasha to the vaccination clinic. Brian drove her to the airport.
Bet she didn't say thank you.
—She didn't. I didn't expect her to.
You don't expect much from her. Does she surprise you?

BITTERSWEET COFFEE

A 20-YEAR-OLD Sasha stands in the frame of our doorless kitchen entrance, the amulet that was Annie's gift to her 17 years ago again dangling around her neck. Clearly there's been a major reconciliation—effected by the gift of the dildo or something else, I don't know.

I'm glad to see it there.

I'm somewhat perturbed… or curious… about how it was found. Did you not deposit it in your sex toy drawer?
—That was ten years ago. I fixed Sasha's chain, and put it in a drawer in her room, a few months later. Alexandra's necklace is also in her room. In the original box.
Does Alexandra know where it is?
—No.
You are a therapist's wet dream. Also, an artist's. But I suspect a mother-daughter moment is around the corner and, as my cock's going soft, I'm going to take this opportunity to avoid friction burn. Tell me this next part in the bathroom. In the shower, or maybe we'll fill the bath. Come…

"What are you doing?" she asks.

I'm sitting at the kitchen table buried in papers. It's the last day of Alexandra's summer vacation and I'm home, taking the day off, but not.

I look at the stacks of affidavits, binders of evidence, research notes from piss-brained associates.

"I'm looking for a lie," I say.

I should ask her how she is. I don't.

I tell myself that it's because I want to respect her privacy, but the truth is, I'm afraid. I don't want to know. I'm a coward. I'm a terrible stepmother.

After all these years... I still don't love her.

"Want a coffee?" she says, walks over to the stove, puts on the kettle before I say a word.

I hesitate. Nod.

Realize that in the 15 years we've been in each other's lives, Sasha and I have never shared a cup of coffee.

And that tells you... everything.

My ritual-less life craves rituals; I know this. I know the five things I do before breakfast, no matter where and with whom, are an attempt to create ritual, structure, comfort in chaos.

What five things do you do before breakfast? And how many of them are dirty?
—None of your business, not part of the story.
Then why bring it up?

My coffee rituals are part of that—they are also the way I commune and connect with people I have, want in my life. They are sometimes the only way I connect with people I'm not fucking.

Now that is also very interesting... and also has me recounting how many times I had to fuck you before you drank coffee with me in the morning.
—I rarely stay till the morning.
You did last time. You will tonight.
—You're making me self-conscious.
Apologies. I'll lather you. And not interrupt. I promise.

When my relationship with Brian progresses from just fucking in his office to spending non-naked time together, it's all about coffee. We meet, first at a campus coffee shop, so innocent, right, just coffee? Then at the one further away from the law building. Then at the one off-campus—we meet, kiss, talk, drink our first cup and grab our refills for take-out. Walk to the university in delicious closeness.

When I remember those moments, I wonder, is Brian more interesting back then? Or does he try harder? Or am I just easier to impress? Or maybe, really, I am in love, it's as simple as that.

Sometimes, when we're on our way to his office, to fuck, getting coffee and the walk that follows, coffee cups in hand, becomes foreplay.

The first time we have coffee together in the morning—terrible, terrible hotel coffee, in an unsexy, unromantic Convention Centre hotel—I almost come with the first sip, and I think that maybe I love him.

After we start living together, after Zia leaves him, and after I know I do not love him but will have to marry him, I get up every morning however early he has to—fuck, why does he keep on choosing to teach 8 a.m. classes?—and make him coffee, have coffee with him.

When I return to the law firm full-time and my workaholic mentor demands I be in the office at 7 a.m. sharp—6:30 preferably, because Toronto, New York, time zones—I find myself getting up alone, drinking coffee alone. It does not occur to Brian to get up with me and I am too proud, too angry to ask him…

That is probably the point at which I stop trying to love him.

Zia invites me out for coffee intermittently—during the brief periods she's speaking to me and "trying to do what's best for Destiny" and I always say no.

No having coffee with the enemy.

No having coffee with Annie—I remember the awful green tea I drank the last time I saw her with distaste.

And shame?
—Yes.

I watch Sasha make the coffee.

I wonder if she knows something big is about to happen.

I wonder if she is here to make another revelation. I wonder if there is anything left with which to shock us.

"I've just pierced my clitoral hood."

"I'm getting a tattoo on my forehead, want to see the art?"

"I had an abortion last week. I thought you should know."

"I tried heroin last night."

All the announcements, delivered in the past by Sasha to her parents—and me. In this house.

In Brian's study.
—Yes.

It occurs to me that perhaps they always happen here not just because this is the place where she can hit Brian and Zia at the same time—I'm an unsatisfactory, unnecessary target,

I just happen to be there—but because this is, ultimately, her safe place. Zia must behave better, in front of witnesses. Maybe?

She can run away and lock herself in her bedroom in this house, and no one will pry her out?

But there are no witnesses today. Just the two of us. Brian has left for his office at the university, "a few things to catch up on before the semester starts," he says. I nod, shrug, don't care.

Alexandra is still asleep, upstairs.

Sasha pours our coffee. Adds cream and cinnamon to mine. I'm shocked. How did she know? I have no idea how she takes hers. I look.

Black.

She carries the cups to the table. I move a binder over so there's room for her cup. Put mine on a liar's affidavit. Gasp—because I see the lie... I've won. I've just won. It's exhilarating. The exhilaration gives me courage and I raise my head and meet Sasha's eyes.

And I smile.

The first sip of each cup of coffee—scalding hot, bitter and sweet, dark and enlivening—remains one of the most sensual, intimate experiences of my life.

I share it with Sasha.

And for the first time in 15 years, I ask...

"What's going on?"

Like every adult—parent—who asks the question, I am unprepared for the silence that follows. I've asked... surely, now, she will tell? But she doesn't. There is silence, long silence.

But there is also coffee. And so, we drink.

"I don't love music, did you know that?" Sasha says abruptly. Is she, like me, too conscious that something momentous is happening? That this is... our *first* cup?

Or is it… just a cup? Just coffee?

"Actually, I don't like it at all," she says.

I nod. Sasha's surprised. But there have been no rock star posters on her walls, no loud music blaring from her room ever.

Had there been, Zia would not have walked in on her and her first lover when she heard their happy noises.

—You said you wouldn't interrupt.

I'm a liar. But go on. I'll try to interrupt only in the important places.

Destiny is the daughter of an angry, controlling woman and a weak, selfish, self-indulgent man. No wonder she's fucked up. But then, are we not all.

Sasha is the daughter of a bitter, lost woman and a confused, lost man. I think her odds are better.

So there she is, at the kitchen table, steaming hot coffee in front of her. In front of me.

I am totally freaked out.

I breathe.

Take a sip of coffee.

Wait for the bad news. What will it be?

"I'm pregnant."

Or…

"I have gonorrhea."

Or…

"I'm really worried about Annie."

What? That, I did not expect.

"What?"

"I'm really worried about Annie," Sasha repeats. "Have you not noticed how different she is lately?"

"Different?" I repeat. Swirl a spoon in my coffee.

I think of all the "I'm worried about Sasha" conversations I've had with Annie over the years. And I'm oddly grateful for this one. Because it shows that... Sasha is neither as selfish as Brian nor as narcissistic as Zia. I realize in a spark of sudden, painful insight that part of my reason for maintaining a distance from my stepdaughter is my dislike, intense, of her parents.

One of whom is my husband.

Fuck.

Sasha fingers the kitschy bead chain on which hangs the sparkling jewel heart she calls her amulet. I'm shocked by how happy I am to see it there.

I'm not.

—You said you wouldn't interrupt.

I said I'd try. And I'd do it only at the important parts. And this is important. You know that, right?

"She keeps on calling me, texting me, giving me things," Sasha says. I raise my eyebrows.

"Does she not always?" I say. "You and your godmother have always been very close."

"It's different," Sasha says. Pauses. "I'm not sure how to express it. It's different."

She gets up, paces the length of the kitchen.

"Anxious," she says finally. "It's anxious. Desperate. Like... she's running out of time."

I don't know what to say.

"Like she's sick," Sasha says. "You know? Like... like she's sick."

And she looks at me like a scared child.

"I haven't really noticed," I say. I lie.

Sasha catches my undertone.

"You have," she says. "You have."

All right. I have.

More. You've drawn conclusions. You think she's having an
affair, and you think she's planning to leave her husband.
—Well. Yes. But I've taken no actions.
Liar.
—I have not. What are you talking about?
All right, not actions. But you are changed: you're unsettled.
At some level, I bet, curious. Concerned.
—No. Neither.
Such a liar. But keep your delusions, for a while longer,
anyway.

"She has not said anything to me," I say. "But then, you know, she wouldn't."

I don't elaborate. I leave it there, I let it hang. I let Sasha have the thought that I'm not the sort of person one tells things to. That she's never told me things.

I look at my stepdaughter, directly. She is young, and therefore, beautiful. Apart from the piercings and tattoos, she is unadorned, her face bare of make up, her hair cut stark. Her clothes are less punk and Goth and more yoga and Zen.

Is she the sort of person one tells things to?

I imagine Zia telling her things, angry things, bitter things, things no child should ever hear, and certainly not about her father.

Who, for all his faults, loves her. I know this, I credit this, even though I don't love him.

I try to imagine Annie confiding in Sasha. That's easy too. But then, imagining Annie confiding, in confession, spilling her guts out, opening her heart—so easy. She is artless even when she is trying to be artful. Transparent in her desires. I know that right now, she is full of things she wants to reveal.

If she looks like that to me, who prefers to be as disconnected from her as possible, how much more transparent she must appear to Sasha, whom she loves and who loves her...

"Has she talked to you? About anything?" I ask Sasha. Sasha shakes her head.

"She wouldn't," she says, and that surprises me. "She wouldn't...." she pauses, "she wouldn't burden me," she says finally. Her cheeks burn. We both know that statement is an indictment of her mother. Who has burdened Sasha with everything.

"I thought she might talk to you," Sasha says. "I think she really needs to. To talk to someone."

"She wouldn't," I say. "She hasn't. She really is more likely to talk to your mother."

"She won't. Not if it's something big, important." And again, red cheeks.

And a plea:

"Will you talk to her?"

I don't want to.

I don't want to care about Annie's angst, affair, or the potential end of her marriage.

"Do you remember," Sasha says, "when you put me in therapy?"

"Which time?" I ask. I try to make it into a joke. I shouldn't. It was only twice.

"I think you saved my life," Sasha says. I nod. I'm pretty sure I did too. Or at least prolonged it, long enough for her to save herself.

"Sometimes, talking to someone, being asked by someone who cares..." Sasha's voice trails off. She's not comfortable in the role she is playing here. She is not comfortable talking to me. But she loves Annie. And so, she is daring.

I can see… Alexandra talking to her. I can see her coming to me after. I can hear her saying, "I'm worried about Alexandra." I want that to happen, if it must…

I take another sip of coffee.

"I will try," I say. "But I don't know… I don't know if it will do any good."

"Thank you," Sasha says.

Finishes her coffee.

Rinses her cup and mine.

Leaves.

And that is that.

WORDS ON THE SCREEN

I SUSPECT I plan to deal with Sasha's request by avoiding
Annie. Not responding to her texts.

Leaving her standing outside my front door as she
repeatedly rings the doorbell.

Fuck, do you really?
—Not for long. But yes. For two, three rings? I'm
afraid to open the door. I'm afraid to start the
conversation.

I open the door slowly, reluctantly.

*Do you know what I love? That there is no doubt in you
that, if you see her, you must ask.*
—What?
*It doesn't occur to you to not do what your stepdaughter
asked you to do. I mean, once you're face to face with your
sister-in-law. Although, apparently, so long as there's a door
between you...*
—Fuck you. You don't know... Anyway. I promised. I
know I have to do it...

But I don't know what to say...

"Hello, come in," strikes me as a good beginning.
—Well. As it is, it's not necessary. Annie speaks first.

"Elizabeth," she says. "Elizabeth, I'm sorry, I didn't know where else to go."

And I realize—her eyes are on fire, and her face streaked with tears, and she's shaking. And I think something horrible must have happened. That Julian is dead or their house burned down, or—fuck, I know how badly she wants a baby, did she conceive and miscarry? Or...

Who the fuck is Julian?
—Brian's brother. Didn't I say that was his name?
You may have. If so, I've forgotten it.
—Well. That's typical—not of you. But of Julian. I forget too...
Julian. Brian's brother. Forgettable. But not dead?
—Not dead.

"Elizabeth," she says. "Please... Oh, god. I want to die."

I move with her as she comes across the threshold. "Bathroom," I say. "Let's go to the bathroom. Clean your face." She follows me—or I follow her—she knows this house as well as I do. Bathroom. I position her in front of the sink. Turn the taps on for her. Wait for her to splash water on her face—but she doesn't. She stares at herself in the mirror.

"What the fuck is wrong with me?" she whispers. "What the fuck is wrong with me?" And, she tilts forward, then slumps, and there she is, sitting on the bathroom floor, her forehead touching the cold base of the pedestal sink.

"What's wrong with me?" she asks, and looks up at me.

I am towering above her, and I know that's wrong. I bend. Crouch. Squat. Finally, sit down beside her.

Should I ask? I don't want to, I don't know how. But I know she needs to tell me, and that I must hear.

I wait for her to speak.

There is silence, for a long, long time.

"He doesn't want me," she says finally.

I know she's not talking about Julian. Although I'm not sure she knows I know.

She does.

"He doesn't want me," she says again, voice like a small child's. It's awful. And she is so... broken, crumpled. She is sitting opposite me, but it seems to me that she is laying in a ball on the floor. Trampled. I don't think I have ever seen a broken heart before and I reach for her. And for the first time in our 15-year relationship, draw her into a genuine embrace. Hold her. Feel her tears on my cheek and neck. Struggle to think how I can comfort her.

You can't.
—No. But I want to. For the first time, ever—with Annie, I mean—I want to.

She starts to talk through her tears, and the words flow, and none of it makes sense, disjointed, broken. I struggle to decipher her meaning, then decide it doesn't matter, and I just hold her, as I would Alexandra.

(As I've never held Sasha.)

As no one has ever held you?
—Fuck. Off.

The first thing I hear is her calling me Liz, which she never does, what the fuck, why the familiarity? —"And the worst of it, Liz? The worst of it? None of it was real. Ever. None of it was real."

"Of course it was real," I say. "It doesn't matter if it's over. It *was*. It existed, it can't be undone, just because it's over." This, I know.

And I know it's not what she needs or wants to hear. But what does she need? Clichés, platitudes. Truths.

I have nothing.

So. "Of course it was real," I repeat.

She laughs. A horrible, horrible laugh. "It wasn't real," she says again. "It was never real. It was just... I was Internet porn that talked back. That's all I was. That's all I feel like. And I feel so used. And..." she pauses, falters, looks at me in desperation, "not in a good way."

The embrace feels awkward now, and I'm relieved when she ends it.

"Let me show you." She sits up, stands up. The water is still running from the tap in the sink and she reaches for it, splashes it onto her face. Gets it all over her coat, scarf. Turns it off—turns to me, phone in hand. Fumbles with it for a minute. Scrolls back, back...

"Look," she says, thrusting the phone at me.

I take it. Words on a screen. Text messages. My eyes don't want to focus. When they do, sentences jump out at me, disjointed still. "What are you wearing?" "What are you doing?" "What do you want?" "I'm willing to sin..." "Tell me..."

Annie's responses, fulsome, full-blown. Castles in the air, romantic fantasies.

I look away from the screen and look at Annie.

"I should not be reading this," I say.

"Please," she says. "Please. Read it. I need someone else to... I need someone else to see..."

I don't understand. But I never do. So I read.

163

The romantic fantasies get sexier, more direct.

Dirtier?
—I suppose.

The lovers—Annie and her lover—play out, in text, elaborate scenes, meetings. In a sauna. In his office. In her classroom. Theatre lobby. Hot tubs and champagne and rose petals, and an edge of danger, exhibitionism. Fantasized encounters under the moonlight in an urban park. A hike through the woods...

I look away.

"Annie," I say. Stop.

"Dozens of conversations like this. Hundreds, actually," Annie says. "Hundreds. So fucking real to me. So fucking real. And in the end? What was it? Nothing, nothing. Words on a screen. Stupid, escapist fantasy. And I... I fell in love with it. With him."

I don't understand.

"It wasn't real," Annie says again. "That's all it was. It was just fucking words on the screen. The love of my life. That turned my life upside down, shook me, stripped me, rebuilt me, destroyed me, saved me... was everything to me. And it was nothing, nothing. Words on a screen. Escapist fantasy, lies. What the fuck is wrong with me?"

What do I say to that?

"I don't understand," I say.

"You never do," she says. "I'm sorry, Liz, I'm sorry. I'm..." The tears come again, and I don't understand a lot of things, but I understand shame, and she is ashamed. But she needs to tell someone, she needs someone to hear if not understand, and so she tells me.

How it wasn't real. How it was just words on the screen.

"We would plan all these meetings," she says. "And at the last minute, always something. Work. Wife. Sick child. Fuck, life. Always... Nothing ever worked out, and how stupid was I, I thought... I believed everything. I thought it was just bad luck, you know? It seemed... it seemed, he wanted me so much..." I want to ask her, who, how did they meet, then realize the initial meeting, hook up was probably on a dating site—where the hell else do people meet these days? I want to ask her which one, but does it matter? There are so many. And I know I *want* to ask these questions because they don't matter, they will keep her from telling me what does.

I don't ask anything.

I don't need to ask her why. I know Julian.

Julian. The man behind the camera, the invisible husband.
—Yes.

The presence of Julian, the absence of Julian. I suspect she has been in a marriage-of-one for years.

Surprisingly insightful.
—I am very insightful. I just prefer not to have insight and intimacy forced onto me.
Do you know, for the first time, I am a little afraid of you.

"Please, read," Annie says through her tears. "Be my... fuck... what?"

Witness.
—Witness.

I turn back to the phone and I scroll through Annie's love affair.

It tears me apart.

The thing about fantasy—about words on the screen—is that every risk is imaginary. There is only excitement. The other hikers don't walk in on you, don't see a white flaccid ass shaking as it thrusts. They come upon the scene at the perfect moment—when she's come, and he's come, and her shirt is pulled down and his pants are done up, and maybe they're disheveled and maybe it looks suspicious—maybe—but that's hot, and it's all OK. Everything is OK.

There is no penalty.

There is always a happy ending.

I say something like this, badly, to Annie.

"So you're saying... you *are* saying, none of it was real," she says. Voice wooden, numb. "That's what he said. It was just a game, Annie. Play. Enjoy. We were having fun, weren't we? We didn't ever fuck. We didn't even make out or *meet* for fuck's sake. That was the point, Annie. No guilt, no harm, Annie. We didn't do anything to risk our real lives—my marriage, yours. Everything's fine, everything's fine..."

She sobs.

"Except it's not, it's not. Fuck, for me, it was the greatest love affair of my life. Stupid, stupid me."

I'm inclined to agree.

I can't decide if I ought to leave her alone on the bathroom floor. Does she need comfort, or does she want privacy? Or if she wants comfort, how the fuck am I supposed to give it?

But it's Annie, and she knows exactly what she wants, and she asks for it.

"Can you read a few more things, read the end," she says. "I know you don't want to. Fuck, Elizabeth, I know you don't want to. I just need... I need someone else to see. To know. I need it to be not just in my head."

I sit beside her. And I read while she cries, the artful mutual seductions, the unapologetic dirty sexting, playful exchanges. Shared experiences of ordinary moments—the half-naked and then more-naked selfies and his cum shots—what is it about men's obsession with photographing their cocks?

It's precisely the same as women's obsession with photographing their faces. Our version of the selfie, that's all.
—Fucking seriously?
Fucking seriously. It's the most beautiful thing about us, what we're most proud of. And most insecure about.

—interspersed with photographs, from Annie, of her garden, her art, beautiful things she notices as she moves through her days...

He loves, lauds all of it, encourages her to share, strip more, expose herself to him completely. Gives her virtually nothing of himself in return—what the fuck does she fall in love with? He shows her nothing but her own reflection.

Nothing of the man behind the words on the screen.

I see it; how can she not?

He gives her his cum shots. It's the ultimate tribute.
—Worthless. Pointless. Not real.
I understand, suddenly, why all our texting exchanges are so tepid. We'll have to work on that.
—We won't.

He ends it suddenly, the callowness of the last cut dressed up in pretty words, selfishness and fear masquerading as nobility, betraying conventionality. "Cracks in my real life... you mean too much to me... my daughter... I can't do both… I can't be the lover I want to be to you and the husband and father I need to be… Never stop wanting you… that's the problem…"

She pleads. The artlessness, nakedness of her desire, her love embarrass me. My cheeks burn—my mind screams, "What the fuck is wrong with you, why, how, could you say such things?"

Because you never would.
—I never would. And I'm appalled, appalled.
But you feel her pain.
—So fucking acutely, it feels like my own…

The last series of messages, from days, weeks ago, to which there is no response, which, I guess, ends the saga, the affair, is from her:

"I suppose the most unforgivable thing here is that I don't want you to be a faithful husband, a *good* husband."

"The only thing that keeps me on this side of sanity is knowing I want you to be a good father."

"All I want is for you to be my lover."

"The perverse game I play with myself late at night is convincing myself that the two are not incompatible. Surely. Can you not be both? Can you not be both?"

The text goes on like this, for paragraphs, and I stare at it in horror. I get… fuck, I don't know what it is. It's like a flashback, except of feelings I never actually experienced in the first place. But should have. I'm 25, and there's a photograph of a little girl on Brian's desk and I don't give a fuck, I don't even notice…

And I am horrified.

I start to weep with Annie.

And I can't stop. She calms down enough to get up, wash her face, and leave. I stay crumpled on the bathroom floor until my phone pings and tells me it's time to pick up Alexandra from choir.

Elizabeth...
—Don't. Just fucking let me recover.
Here. Have a towel. Do you want to sit on the bathroom floor with me?
—Don't you mock me.
Never. Lover. Never.

ADDICTIONS

IT'S BECAUSE OF Annie's breakdown, heartbreak, whatever that I agree to another coffee shop "women of the family" meeting the next Monday after work. At Vendome this time, because both Annie and I are too embarrassed to go to Café Blanca again.

Fuck no. Not another book club session.
—No book.
Just four women bitching. Jesus.
—I don't have to tell this story at all.
Yes, you do. We've finally cracked your armour. Let's see what oozes out.

Zia's there when I walk in, and I see that she—she of the red cocktail dresses, designer purses, and two-hour make-up sessions—is wearing a T-shirt.

White, stark, the lettering hot pink. "Oprah didn't die for your sins," it reads. And there's a hot pink ribbon.

And I notice... her eyes are red and naked and that ashen olive I see is her natural skin without artful foundation. If she's wearing yoga pants, the world has ended.

I look. She's not. Shorts, tight, showing off the type of legs women in their twenties cannot fathom can belong to a woman on the edge of menopause. Sandals. Painted toes.

All is not lost.

She sees me looking at her shorts and snarls again.

I wish Annie, Sasha, either, both, would hurry up and arrive.

I slide into the chair opposite her—because it's not one of the chairs beside her.

"What?" she snarls again. Apparently, I'm still looking. I avert my eyes from her legs. And what? Do I say anything? Do I say, "I've never seen you without make-up. Or in a T-shirt."

A friend would say, "What's wrong?" because, clearly, something is.

But we are not friends.

"What do you want to drink?" I ask.

"A gin and tonic," she says. "I desperately want a gin and tonic. A beer. A glass of wine. Skip the glass. Give me the bottle. Fucking anti-freeze."

I'm rigid.

"Coffee, black, then," I say.

It's at least five years since we—Brian and Annie, really, I hid upstairs with Alexandra for the most part, trying not to vomit—have had to talk Zia off this particular ledge.

I order coffee for her. Earl Grey tea for me. Then add a chocolate brownie, carrot cake, and almond croissant to the mix. When I return with the offerings to the table, Zia does not say thank you. She gulps the coffee and I see it scald her mouth. Then breaks off a piece of the croissant.

"Are you trying to make me get fat?" she says, and it's not a joke, it's an accusation.

"Yes," I say. "I want you to get fat. When you finish these, I'll get you more. I want you to look grotesque. Ugly. Repellant."

She breaks off a piece of the brownie.

"I want to cram this thing whole into my mouth and swallow it without chewing," she says. "I want to go out to a tawdry hotel bar, drink, and wake up in bed with a stranger. I want to drag my 30-year-old house painter into my bedroom. I want…"

"You're painting your condo?" I say, because I want to stop her.

"Yes, Elizabeth, I'm painting my condo. That's the critical piece of information in that statement. I'm painting my condo. Or, if you like, Brian's money is painting my condo. You're painting my condo!" her voice rises and people look at us.

I hate her.

I fucking hate her, and why am I babysitting her?

Where are Sasha and Annie?

I pull out my phone—no messages.

"I'm so fucking sorry I'm boring you," Zia says—no, snarls.

And I look at her and I'm six, 16. Except I'm not. I'm an adult and I should be free and I'm not fucking putting up with this anymore.

"Fuck you, you stupid, selfish cunt," I say. Get up and start walking to the door just as Sasha and Annie are coming in. I'm not sure if Zia is talking behind me or screaming—all I hear is a buzzing in my ears.

But while part of me is 16 and walking out of my mother's life again, the rest is an adult with responsibilities, so I don't brush past Annie and Sasha, but stop. Make myself focus on Annie.

"You need to talk to her," I say. Turn to Sasha, and put a hand on her arm.

"Come with me." It's not a request. I think Zia is screaming, heedless of the coffee shop's other customers—here's another café we can never go to again, how many does that make—but I don't know for sure, there is nothing more than just dull thuds in my skull now. Sasha looks over my shoulder at her mother and her face goes white. I shepherd her outside, almost pushing her.

"What did you say to her?" she demands when we're on the sidewalk. "Why did you upset her?"

Because I'm a cunt.

Actually, I'm going to say that. Because. I am.

And I do.

Sasha flushes. I'm glad to see colour returning to her cheeks; I'm glad she's choosing anger over fear.

Even if it's anger at me.

"Yes, you are," she says. And storms off. Away from the café. Away from her mother.

My work is done.

I wonder if I should text, warn Brian. But no. Annie will do that if she must.

I text Stefan instead.

"I need to be naked in your arms, right now."

Immediate response.

"205 12B Street SW. It's a gallery. Come through the back door, go into the basement."

Yes.

You realize, my lover, sex is your addiction? Your alcohol—your soother—your drug?

—Isn't it everyone's first drug of choice?

No. Not at all. So I'm wondering, what goes wrong when you come to me?

—Does it matter?

Everything matters. But in the moment, what matters most is how I'm going to position you as you tell me about your encounter with Stefan in the art gallery. One, incidentally, that I recognize by the address. A third-rate, mediocre gallery that refused to show my work when I was starting out, and so worthy of nothing but contempt. Redeem it for me. But first... mmmm, here. Like this. Like "Olympia." Legs crossed... so... and as you talk, I will see if I can get them to spread.

—And this is not your addiction?

I judge not. Now talk. I'm getting flaccid again.

I arrive shaking, frazzled. Not aroused, not in the mood, just, oh, so fucking angry. I run into Stefan without seeing him, crash against his body. He starts to explain what he's doing—frames, friend's show, light—I cover his mouth with my hand. "Today, it's about me," I say. "No setting the fucking scene. No foreplay. Fuck me. Break me. Just..."

If he doesn't turn my brain off, right now, right away, I will die. Or at least go mad.

He pulls my trousers down to my knees roughly and thrusts a hand between my legs. "I don't think you're ready," he whispers.

"I don't fucking want to be ready," I would scream if I dared, but I will never scream, I will never sound like her. "Now!"

There isn't a lot of wall real estate in the little dank room, so he pushes me onto the floor. Rams into me. Does what he's told. There's pain, and I close my eyes and I turn off my brain. And maybe I cry.

Bite his shoulder, his hand. Come, in a wave of release that is in no way about pleasure.

He holds me after. "We ruined your suit," he says.

"I don't care," I say. He doesn't ask what happened. I'm grateful.

I read the text from Annie as he watches me dress.

"It's OK. She'll be fine. You did good."

Patronizing bitch. I didn't. I panicked, I ran.

"But you know… we really should get her a boyfriend. It's been way too long. And she's lonely. I think a boyfriend, a love affair is just what she needs."

Because it worked out so well for you?

Jesus, Annie, what the fuck are you thinking?

I am perturbed—massively—by your portrayal of these women, you know. Annie and Zia. Fuck, yourself. It's making me rethink my position on married women.

—And what is your position on married women?

This. That stocking's so useful—come here. Into my lap, pet. And, let's see… face away from me… and hands behind your back…

—I am so uncomfortable.

It's not about your comfort, it's about my desire. And I'm answering your question. My position on married women is—no, I don't want you on my cock, slide forward, at the moment, I just want you uncomfortable and frustrated— my position on married women is that they make the best lovers. They are… comfortable, lover?

—No! I'm….

Good. They are comfortably situated, and frustrated—on the edge, on a constant trigger. They have so much to lose—and so they value what they give—what I take—that much more. And they have a pair of manly arms to comfort them when I am done with them.

—You're a sociopath.

Not at all. I know I will be done with them, and I'm happy that they'll have someone to comfort them. It's much more cruel to break a single woman's heart.

—But when you do break a married woman's heart, you really do shatter it.

Are you talking about Annie? Zia? Or yourself?

—I don't know.

ENABLER

WHEN I WALK into the house, I hear Brian moving around in his office—sorry, study. I see Alexandra's coat and backpack on the floor in the entry way, pick them up mechanically. See Sasha's shoes.

I walk into the kitchen.

"Secondary," Sasha says. Alexandra, sitting at the kitchen table, writes the word down.

I freeze. It should be... what I am seeing should be a tableau that's an intimate, constant picture in a family. The little sister, with her homework spread out on the kitchen table. The big sister, helping her. Maybe prepping supper. There is, on the kitchen counter, evidence of peeled potatoes. Salad.

"Brian did that," Sasha says, following my eyes. Lest I think she did it? (She started calling Brian Brian, and not Dad, sometime around the first piercing.)

I say nothing. I'm still frozen.

"Dumped," Sasha says. And Alexandra writes it down.

"What are you girls doing?" I ask. The plural "girls" sounds strange in my throat. I never use it. I never talk, think about our girls.

Our daughters.

Your daughters.

"I have to make a list of ten words I despise for their ugliness," Alexandra says. "But all I could come up with are swears. And I bet my teacher..." her voice trails off.

"Adultery," I say, without thinking.

"How do you spell that?" Alexandra asks. Sasha letters it out for her. Very carefully not looking at me. Then...

"Divor-cée," she says.

"Divorcée?" I ask. "Not divorce?"

"No," Sasha says. "There's nothing wrong with divorce. Divorcée is the ugly word."

"And how do you feel about cheater?" I ask.

"It's a social construct," she says. "What about liar... No. I always think liar should be an uglier word than it is. You know? Liar is almost too soft. Pretty."

"I don't need pretty, I need ugly," Alexandra says.

"Unicorn," Sasha says. Alexandra starts to protest. "No, go with it," Sasha says. "Tell your teacher it's ironic."

"Alexandra's teacher is going to send her for counseling," I say.

"Then we should make it really good," Sasha says. "That's... five?"

"Five more," I nod.

"Are you guys trying to get me in trouble with my teacher?" Alexandra wails.

"No," I say. "Enabler."

"Doesn't fit the theme," Sasha protests.

"I don't know what it means!" Alexandra wails again.

"It's a great word, your teacher will love it," I tell her. But I don't define it.

"I still don't know what it means," she says. But she writes it down.

"Victim," Sasha says. "No, not victim: victimhood. Way uglier."

I cock my head. Interesting.

"Blame," I say. "Or, blaming. Either one—u-gly." Sasha nods.

"That's eight, counting enabler," Alexandra says. Looks at us, expressively, expectantly.

"Grudge," Sasha says.

"Obligation," I say.

We look at each other over Alexandra's bent head.

"Enabler?" Sasha says. "Really?"

"One of the ugliest words I know," I say.

"Enabler?" she says again.

"Enabler," I echo. Pause. "But… don't forget… blame is also a fucking ugly word." My voice trails off. I feel I should say more, but don't know what. I go silent.

"I still don't know what 'enabler' means," Alexandra says. Looks at her list. "But all these words look very ugly."

"Good," I say. "Now go get out of your uniform." She gathers up her books, traipses off. Sasha turns her back on me.

"Are you staying for supper?" I ask her back.

"I don't know," she says. "Are you?"

I nod even though she can't see me.

"Then you should change your clothes before my father fucking sees you," she says.

"I doubt he would notice," I say. Walk out of the kitchen slowly. And if he noticed… would he dare to comment?

Probably not.

Does he?
—He picks them up off our bedroom floor. "Tsk, tsk, these will need to be dry cleaned," he says. Then we talk about Zia, briefly. He thinks everything will be fine, that she caught herself in time.
Do you fuck?

178

—No. I don't want him to touch me. I don't want him to touch me, ever again, and I can't explain to myself why.

Do you still want to fuck Stefan? Or others?

—That is a leading question.

I like to lead. You know that. So follow.

FOOLISH COUGAR

THE THING ABOUT life that's hugely inconvenient is that most milestones, seminal moments—really aren't. Some of them look like it…

You walking in, mostly naked, on Brian's mostly naked wife, for example…
—That's a bad example—that was an actual milestone that led to the dissolution of her marriage and the beginning of mine…
I suppose that's a way of telling me to leave the telling of the story to you?

…but they aren't, not really. In retrospect, they all become just parts of the past, which is never truly over, because it just keeps on fucking up the present and pre-determining the course of the future.

Are you saying all the milestones you're telling me about don't matter?
—No. I think what I'm trying to say is that they seem to matter so much when they happen… and then they kind of fizzle. And you keep on expecting for them to have changed everything… but they haven't. Not really. Life just goes on.

And that's what happens. Life just goes on. I go to work. Alexandra goes to school. Sasha finds another job, but doesn't yet move out. As a waitress, which you'd think would please Zia, but it doesn't, of course, because it's in a dodgy bar, and it's not the sort of job that the daughter of a law professor and the woman supported by his alimony should have.

Bitter, a little?
—Fuck, yes. Bitter, a lot.

Brian perks up a little, as he always does at the beginning of a new semester. Zia's Zia, hating me, loving Sasha, making everyone's lives as uncomfortable as possible and getting away with it, because, we are all enablers, of one thing if not the other.

Annie can't stop crying.

And she's not eating.

Every time I see her, her eyes are red and swollen. And her clothes don't fit. I tell Sasha I've talked to her, and she's fine, she's not sick, a little stressed, you know, life. Sasha doesn't believe me. I'm not surprised. She's still worried about Annie, and I suppose so am I.

I even text her. "How are you?"

She responds, "I want to die." She follows with, "I won't. Don't fucking go on suicide watch for me. But don't make me fucking lie to you at least."

I text back, "OK."

One day, Julian texts me.

"Elizabeth. I was wondering if you've talked with Annie lately."

I don't write him back. What could I possibly say?

But when Annie texts me and asks me if I will go with her to a Pride event, a Hot Mess Party at the Republic, to "support Sasha, who really wants us to come," I don't ask a lot of questions, just say yes. And her eyes are swollen, and her clothes are too loose, but she's grimly determined to have fun, and so I follow her into the nightclub line-up and look, in mild dismay, at the drunk 20-year-olds surrounding us.

"Christ, you didn't tell me we were going to act like we're 21," I tell Annie. She laughs, and it's a fake laugh, but it's a laugh, so that's something. Then she points at the boy-child in line ahead of us, and laughs again.

He's wearing those awful pants, the ones where the belt clinches really below the butt, and the wearer's buttocks— usually clad in unattractive men's boxer shorts, because there is no such thing as attractive men's boxer shorts—are flaunting themselves.

Fuck, I know. The second most important reason I'm grateful to not be 18 or even 28. Missed that fashion horror show.
—What's the first?
Incredible staying power.

"I'm going to pull his pants up," Annie whispers and tugs on the belt loop.

"Hey!" he turns around. "Those are for pulling down, not pulling up." Then he looks at her and then me. Wiggles his ass.

"Do you like that?" he says.

"No, not really," I say as Annie turns the colour of a ripe tomato. "They do absolutely nothing for me."

"That's because you're a lesbian," he says. I shrug.

"Probably," I say.

"Ooh, baby, snap," he high fives me.

I feel odd, like I'm in a *Twilight Zone* episode. His boyfriend laughs and then reaches over and squeezes his boxer-short clad—the pattern is cherries and hearts—butt cheeks.

Suddenly, I understand my boxer short antipathy. I'm the wrong demographic. It's not for the girls. It's for the boys.

I wonder if straight men know this.

I wonder if Sasha really wants us to be here? As I look at Annie, jittery, high-energy, anxious—not crying, but fuck, clearly on the verge of tears—I suspect Sasha couldn't care less—or, more likely, will be embarrassed by our presence if she sees us. I suspect Annie's broken heart has propelled her into a full-on midlife crisis…

Or her midlife crisis propelled her into a broken heart?

…and she wants to drink and grind ass—or at least dance. With abandon. I suspect Zia, who scoffed and snorted at the suggestion, and is not here, is, in this case, the wise one.

We wait in line and it does not move. And it's cold. Annie, who left her coat in the car and is wearing a tank top, is shivering.

Cherry Boxers' boyfriend offers her his "cardigan." It reeks of beer. And pot. Annie declines.

"Good," he says. "I didn't really want to lend it to you. And this way, I get the best of both worlds. I've offered—but I get to stay warm."

He and Cherry Boxers howl. Start making out.

I sigh. I am out of my element—we are out of our element—and I'm not relishing it.

It's not even that we're too old. It's Pride Weekend, and so this line up is full of everyone from teens through to toothless grandpas. Cherry Boxers is barely 20—but his boyfriend's at least ten years older than I am. More.

It's that we're too straight. Too... lame. Annie, I think, might pass a visual. Her tank top is camp, her jeans right, and she's wearing combat boot style shoes—I realize Sasha would tell me I'm stereotyping, but whatever. But even though I'm wearing more or less the same thing under my coat, tank, jeans, Fluevogs—I look straight, square, dull.

A middle-aged lawyer playing dress up. Not in my skin. Out of place. In this atmosphere of play, excess, celebration, I feel apart.

And I don't want to be here. I don't want Sasha to feel I'm trespassing on her world. I don't want to watch Annie try so hard to have fun.

I want to lie naked on the floor of Stefan's studio while he splatters paint on me... I spin the fantasy as the line moves, slowly, and we're finally pushed into the crowded, stinky, loud club.

Now I feel old.

Annie takes off for the dance floor and tries to pull me after her. I mime drinking and go to the bar. Order a club soda and lime. Turn around to see Cherry Boxers with his arm wrapped around an equally young boy, whom he tries to press into my arms. It's too loud to catch his name, all I hear is "...fuck a dyke." I raise my eyebrows. "What?" I shout. The boy leans in to me. "I've got a bucket list for these things," he shouts into my ear. "One of the things on it is I want to fuck a dyke!"

Awesome. I evade the hand going for my ass.

"Not actually a dyke," I shout at him.

"Haven't done a straight chick in a while either!" he shouts.

What the fuck? I'm not sure who I hate more at this moment for putting me into this situation—Sasha, for—

fuck, what? Being gay and being at this thing? Or Annie, for making me feel guilty and worried and…

I love it. I'm already picturing you in a nightclub washroom on your knees.
—It's good to have fantasies.
Not gonna happen?

The boy keeps on rubbing against me, and I keep on evading, and I suppose it looks like we're dancing. He might even think we are.

"So what do you like?" he asks.

I think, as if it's a serious question that matters.

"Variety," I finally say. Although I'm not sure that's true.

"I do too. Hey. You're variety—I haven't done a woman in forever. And I'm variety. Bet you haven't been with a gay boy for a while, if ever. I'm variety. Come downstairs and suck my cock."

"Does that actually work on anyone?"

"Sometimes. Yes? Let's go." He grabs my hand. I shake it off.

"I have no interest in sucking your cock," I say.

"Well, what are you interested in?" he asks.

Would I? Could I? I wouldn't, because this is not the type of risk I take. Nightclubs, washrooms, barely legal but so promiscuous, what-could-they-be-infected-with strangers? Not my thing.

I'm rather glad, actually…

"You could lick my pussy," I say, but I don't mean it. It's a game. "Or you could finger fuck me. Mmmm, maybe while we're standing at the bar."

I'm playing a role. The woman who says this, who would do this, here, I'm not.

"You would be so horribly disappointed," he says. "I have no practice. And so, horrible technique."

"Then maybe we should just dance," I offer, because in that moment, in his humility and honesty, I quite like him.

"No, I really want to get fucked or sucked tonight," he says. "I'm gonna keep on hunting."

"Good luck," I say. He leans into an assumed embrace. Kisses my cheek.

"Good luck in your pursuit of variety," he says.

Fuck. I wish you had fucked him. I can see it. On your knees in the filthy washroom, a fat cock in your mouth.

—I wouldn't do that even for you.

You will. It's going on my bucket list. As two items. Item one, mouth-fucking Liz in a dirty nightclub washroom. Item two, telling Liz to mouth-fuck a stranger in a dirty nightclub washroom. Next time you tell this story, you go down on him.

—But that's not what happened.

Right. I keep on forgetting this is autobiography. Continue. What happens next?

—The old embarrass the young.

I shove my way towards the dance floor, but before I get there I get intercepted by Sasha. Who is furious.

"Why are you guys here?" she demands. "And what the fuck is she doing? Elizabeth! Get her off the dance floor and take her home! How fucking drunk is she?" I follow her eyes, and I see, Annie, Annie locked in an embrace with a stranger—not a stranger—oh, with little suck-my-cock boy.

"Get her out of here!" Sasha repeats. "She's embarrassing me!"

I nod. I accept that our very existence embarrasses Sasha; I don't need her to explain to me that she does not want to

186

think of her godmother as either a sexual being or a fallible one, the young never do—that's why it's such a tragedy when their parents fall off their pedestals, as they must.

I push my way to Annie. Start to pull her away from the boy. He pulls her back, shoves me away.

"Sorry, she's my ride," I tell him.

"You're ruining my night, cunt," he says. And there's nothing good-humoured or affectionate about it. Our camaraderie of an hour before is gone. He would hurt me if he could—I give him a measured look, remembering all the physical characteristics I might need for filling out a police report.

I drag Annie out and into the car. She's red. I'm silent. I drop her off home. Her mood is—I don't know. I can't read it.

"I wasn't drinking," she says, as she steps out of the car. "I didn't have a single drink."

"I know," I say, even though I don't know.

"If you could tell Sasha, please," she says. "I didn't have anything to drink. I was stupid without the aid of alcohol."

I nod. Suddenly, I understand.

And, oh, fuck. So does she.

"Liz? I mean, Elizabeth?" she gets back into the car. No. No. We are not going to talk about this.

But this is Annie the obtuse, fuck, how can someone so sensitive be so obtuse...

"I just noticed, I just realized. Do you... do you ever, I mean, do you drink?"

I know she doesn't mean water, coffee, tea. The occasional glass of juice. The celebratory sip of wine... that I don't swallow.

I would think it funny that she just noticed this about me, except that I just noticed this about her. Even though I noticed Zia's long dry stretches and painful backslides long before Brian saw fit to tell me the mother of his first child was a recovering—often slipping, always struggling—alcoholic.

"Life is full of personal choices that are not the concern of nosy relatives," I say.

I'm a cunt, I know. But fuck her and what she needs right now.

I'm tired of it always being about someone else. I'm not telling my story to make her feel better about her story.

I don't want a connection.

I don't want us to be the same. We're not.

My lover, what a lonely path you walk.
—Fuck you. I don't want to tell you that story either.
Don't. Although—lover—you already have, you know. But if it makes you feel better, let's pretend you told me nothing. Pray continue with your most interesting—if heavily censored—narrative.

She's crying as she walks towards her front door.

I think about texting Sasha that I delivered Annie home safe, but I don't know how to phrase it. And it seems wrong. She shouldn't be worrying about her godmother.

Neither, I suppose, should I.

But you do. Even though you're pretending you don't.
—Fuck you. But fine, yes. I do. I've never… I've never felt, suffered as she is suffering. It is horrible to experience, second-hand. I don't know how she will survive it.
You envy her.
—No!
You do. You envy her. Why?
—I don't know.
I think I do. Go on.

NO MORE

BRIAN AND I are trying not to fight over the letter on the dining room table—a request from Zia, via her lawyer, for an increase in her living allowance. We are both lawyers, if not family law experts, and we both know her request is ludicrous, unfounded, and legally fucked. It will be laughed out of court by any judge.

Brian wants to acquiesce to it. Because, peace. Because, we can afford it.

"You mean, I can afford it," I say. Brutally, meaning to wound. I rarely mention how much more money I make than he does. He's not, frankly, privy to just how much more that is.

He flinches.

"Liz…" he implores.

"No more," I say. "It's been 15 fucking years and your daughter is now 20. No more. I'm not cutting her off. I'm just not giving her more."

We lock eyes, and his guilt stares at me. I stare back at it, angry.

I know his guilt almost as well as I know mine, and I know the Zia-bound withdrawals that leave our account every month are his atonement. They have grown in size each year independent of Sasha's age, independence, or prolonged residence in our house. Their size and regularity speak as eloquently to our guilt, respective and joint, as any religious act of contrition.

No more.

"Liz," he repeats. Reaches for the letter.

"No," I say. My hand moves towards his, pauses. Our hands are suspended over the table as Sasha bursts into the dining room.

"Do we have any wooden clothes pins?" she asks. Our anger hangs in the air. I know what I'm angry about. Where his anger is coming from, I'm not sure.

"All I can find is this plastic pastel crap." She's holding a bag of pink, blue, and green clothes pins.

"I didn't even know we had any clothes pins," I say mechanically. Sit down, so I'm not standing and glowering.

"The plastic ones are fine, they'll do the job," Brian says. Sits down as well.

"Not at a kink party, they won't," Sasha says, and storms out of the room.

"Does she say and do these things just to shock us," Brian says. It's not a question, it's a lazy, languid statement to which he doesn't need an answer.

I suppose the clothes pin interjection ends our fight. The steam's gone out of both of us, and neither of us desires conflict, or does conflict particularly well. That, I suppose, is my particular gift as a litigator. I really don't want the punching session in the ring. How can we avoid it?

But once you're in the ring? Or, courtroom?
—I don't lose.

I pick up the letter. "I'll get one of my partners to deal with this," I say. Brian can choose to think I've let him— Zia—win.

190

But you won't.

—Not this time.

What's changed?

—I don't yet know. Don't push ahead of the story. At the moment, it's one of those false milestones…

"I'll drive Sasha to get clothes pins. And, I suppose, to her Halloween kink party," I say as I exit the room. "And on the way, I think, I'll not-so-subtly suggest maybe she should get a fucking driver's license."

Brian's taking Alexandra to choir. He says nothing.

CRASH

TWENTY MINUTES LATER, Sasha and I are sitting in my slightly flattened car, the anti-lock brakes of which have failed, causing me to cause a three-car pile-up on Deerfoot. The police are on their way; an ambulance, mercifully, isn't.

My head is scattered and I feel stupid. The accident is my fault, the result of my carelessness—almost my willfulness. And I'm terrified, I don't like feeling like this—I feel myself unraveling.

And I'm pretty sure it's Annie's fault. What is she triggering in me right now? Why?

And why, after 15 years of successfully not giving a fuck about her, am I now letting her pain tear me apart?

You sure you weren't distracted because you were pissed off at the ex-wife wanting more money?
—Yes. That demand's an annual thing.

I don't want to think about Annie and her suffering, so I try to make myself think about Zia and be angry about Zia. What I manage, instead, is this: I wonder, not for the first time, how Zia feels about Annie's relentless campaign to connect with me. After all, she and Annie were "first."

It was Zia who introduced Annie to Brian's brother, actually. This I know; I do not know how Annie and Zia know each other, how they first meet.

The one time I ask, I'm answered with silence.

And more silence.

Finally:

"It was such a long time ago," Zia says. Does not look at me. Or Annie. "I don't remember." Then, she rallies, her voice booms. "We've known each other for lifetimes, haven't we, darling?"

Annie laughs. Her hands flutter, cover her mouth and eyes. Disconnected and distant though I am, I know I've hit a nerve.

But I don't care enough to pursue it.

Sasha, however, present and angry at her mother over something, everything, does.

"I know," she says. "I'll tell you sometime, Elizabeth."

"You. Will. Not," Zia hisses. Turns the conversation. Annie helps. Sasha stares at her, at me.

I back away, withdraw.

How many years ago was that? Six? Seven?

Oddly enough, Sasha is following the same train of thought.

"Do you remember that?" she asks me. Cars whizz by, heads turn. We're today's spectacle.

"What?" I'm staring out the windshield, too stressed to even curse. I do all the things. Call the police, call Brian to make sure he's picking up Alexandra from choir. ("I always do," he says, defensive; "I know," I say, "just making sure nothing else goes wrong.") I call the insurance company. Give Sasha my cell phone so she can call her date. "She's going to come pick me up from here," she tells me as she gives me back my phone and pockets her dead one. I nod. "That OK?" she asks after a pause. I nod again, then frown.

"You didn't ask," I say. "You made a statement." The lawyer sometimes comes out in the most ridiculous situations.

"Would you rather I stayed with you?" Sasha asks. I'm looking out the window, but I become aware she's looking at me. Turn my head. She's wearing a pirate costume. The eye-patch is pushed up off her face into her hair. I don't know where she was going to put the clothes pins that we haven't bought. Realize I probably don't want to know.

"There's no need," I say. And don't understand why she bites her lip and turns away. And then, I think I do. She doesn't want to stay. Of course not. Who would? She wants to go on her date, to the Halloween costume party. But she wants me to want her to stay.

Everyone wants to feel wanted.
—Yes.

Do I want her to stay?

Her mother, we both know, would not make leaving an option. And a younger Sasha would wail and rail. And stay. Sullen and unhappy. This Sasha? I think she would leave.

Do I want her to stay?

"Of course I would appreciate the company," I say carefully, even though I don't know if it's true. If I was alone in the car, I could put my head on the steering wheel. Slump down. Weep, maybe. I really want to weep, I'm not sure why. Or I could text Stefan and masturbate to his words.

Or I could just close my eyes and disappear into myself.

"But I know you want to go to your party. Go."

"You talk like a robot," Sasha says. Then falls silent. I say nothing either. I close my eyes. Slump over the steering wheel. Let myself feel… exhausted. Angry. Resentful.

Sad.

Disappointed.

So… regretful.

"Do you remember that?" Sasha says again. "When I told you I'd tell you, sometime, how Annie and my mother met?"

You can't nod with your head laying on the steering wheel, so I say, "Yes."

"It was at an AA meeting," Sasha says. Viciously. "They were both drunks. Annie told me, once. When Mom started drinking, again. It was supposed to make me understand her, make me feel sorry for her? I don't know. It just made me hate them both. Drunks."

I say nothing. Because, what can I say? That Sasha's big revelation is no revelation, but a fact of my fucking life? That the one missing piece of information is that Annie and Zia met at AA. Zia's struggle with too much wine and prescription drugs used for not quite the right reasons has been a backstory of my marriage to Brian. An excuse, reason for the irrationality, the screaming. Also, on more than one occasion, the regressions, according to Zia, my fault. Of course.

And yet. Also this. She keeps fighting. She keeps on quitting. Going to meetings that she tells Sasha are book clubs, Avon, fundraisers.

I realize I'm feeling a twinge of compassion for Zia. I'm shocked.

"Do you know what it's like to have an emotionally abusive, fucking drunk for a mother?" Sasha, tired of my silence, demands.

Ha.

What a question.

Actually, I do know. But I won't say so.

I embrace the steering wheel as if it is a lover who can offer me succor and comfort. I want to sink into it, disappear.

I could say... what? "It takes courage to fight that disease." Sounds like something Annie would say, probably has said to Sasha in the past. I have no idea what to say. But I must say something. Sasha's expectation, anticipation of a response is so intense I can almost reach out and touch it.

So.

"She loves you. Very much," I say. Still slumped, but my head turned towards her, so I see the toss of the head and the turn of the chin.

"Love is overrated. It's not enough," the 20-year-old says with the brutality, the clarity of the young. And then, turning back to look at me:

"You don't love me. You don't even love Dad. But you do all the things..."

"Sasha!" a hand knocks on the passenger window. Sasha opens the door and steps out of the car into an embrace. Pokes her head back in.

"Thanks for trying to give me a ride." She sounds ungracious. Does she? Maybe not. She closes the car door with care.

I think I'm going to vomit and I wonder if the fiddleheads I had for lunch will come out curled like snails or ground up into half-digested mush. And it's this focus on the potential contents of my potential puke that lets me pull myself together sufficiently to fill out the police report. Answer the questions.

I don't love her.

I don't love her father.

But I do all the things.

If love is not enough... is *that* enough?

I don't know. As soon as the police are done with me, I call a cab and text Stefan.

"Do you want a muse?"

He writes back: "Immediately. Run every red light."

I don't. But I tell the cab driver to speed, a little.

SUFFERING FOR ART

STEFAN WANTS TO paint me wearing golden ballet shoes, pirouetting under the birch in his garden. It's October and it's yellow and he says the light is a gift from god. I'm torn between a "well, he's the artist" feeling and a "this is stupid" feeling. When he gives me the shoes—so kitschy—the "this is stupid" feeling becomes painted on my face. And when he tells me he wants me naked in the pose, and wearing a blonde wig, my mouth starts to articulate it.

"Sshhh," he closes my lips with a kiss and starts unbuttoning my shirt. I can't form words, because his tongue is in my mouth, and as his fingers unclasp each button, they move to caress my ass, thighs, cunt lips, and I moan. And when I'm naked, he crouches down with me in his arms, and puts the ballet shoes on me while holding me in his lap. He keeps me in his arms while he goes for the wig.

It's intoxicating. I am setting, a prop, and it's intoxicating.

He carries me to the birch and starts arranging the pose, his fingers brushing against my nipples, my clit, tracing the curve of each ass cheek.

"Wet?" he whispers in my ear and tongues it. "I want you dripping through the pose."

"Cold," I moan. It's almost the end of October, and the sunlight he covets is not giving me much warmth.

He slides a finger inside me.

"Wet," he corrects. "Suffer for my art. I'll warm you up later."

That works on you, lover? I'm so disappointed.
—Perhaps I'm not fully conveying the eroticism of the situation.
Clearly. Try harder.

He doesn't start to paint: he photographs first—to capture the light, he explains. Then sketches. And then, starts to throw paint at the canvas. But by that point I understand that it's not about the painting for him. The painting's the afterthought. The foreplay with the model is the purpose. *That's* his art.

As I stand there, feet cold, nipples erect—"suffering for his art"—I already know that the sex, when it comes, will be anti-climactic. The high point was being stripped naked, posed.

I ponder leaving, mid-pose, before he fucks me.

Tell me you do.
—Not that time. But it doesn't last much longer.

PLAYING CUPID

I DECIDE TO give Stefan to Zia, oh, when? He keeps on working on that birch painting: I keep on having to pose for it in the wig and the ballet slippers, although mercifully no longer outside, and it starts to piss me off. There's only so much of the derivative, pretentious artist I can take.

I'll keep that in mind. Now bend over. Like this. Continue.

I'm not sure how or why the veneer wears off. Maybe it starts with the art: it starts to look so simplistic, uninspired. And always, unfinished. I only loved the art while I loved the artist, and suddenly I am done, and the desire and appreciation of both gone. Completely. I have no idea why, I'm just empty. Last time I was here, I could not wait for his mouth, his hands.

I'm done.

I have no idea what has changed.

I study him as he works, the incline of his shoulders. The long hair strikes me as pretentious. The beard, tacky. The bare feet, with their paint-splattered, yellowing toenails repel me.

And the moment he starts mumbling that his marriage is in trouble, it's over. I know he's looking for a new sugar momma, and that will not be me. He tells me, doe-eyes gazing into mine, that his wife is asking for a divorce. Then his lips begin to work their way down my torso.

The idea of giving him to Zia comes to me as he bites my shoulder and slides a finger into my ass…

Like that?
—Ah…

I am at that moment, both pissed off at Zia, and sorry for her—and so ashamed of myself… and I am so tired of… everything, really. I'm tired of having her in my life. I'm tired of her continued anger, resentment. I'm tired that, 15 years later, I'm still the villain. And so's Brian. I'm tired that she's not over it. I'm tired of the battles over Sasha. Over money.

You don't raise her living allowance.
—I don't raise her already outrageously generous living allowance, no.

I'm tired of everything.

As Stefan finally puts down the paint brush and pushes me on the floor, I decide I'm tired of sex that never lives up to the promise of the build-up.

With Stefan on top me, his swollen cock inside me, the pounding steady and yet monotonous, I decide that what Zia needs is a 30-something lover with a big ego, a decent-sized cock, and limited ambition.

I decide the best way to get rid of Stefan is to introduce him to my husband's ex-wife.

I decide that she will glory in the act of taking away my lover.

I decide, as he groans, thrusts, but doesn't quite come, that I am clearly insane.

It's stupid.

It's insulting and demeaning to them both.

It's unforgivable.

But I decide to do it anyway.

"Stefan?" I whisper, as his fingers replace his cock. "There's someone I know who I think you should meet."

Oh, Elizabeth. Oh, Elizabeth. I don't quite know how this will end, but I no longer think it's all your sister-in-law's fault.

—Well. This specific part isn't, no. Although she's the one who plants the seed... She's the one who wants to play Cupid for Zia.

And you decide to use the opportunity to unload a lover who might be shopping for a... what did you say? Sugar momma? My Liz. Never was I so glad I sold out. Shall we explore your horror of dependent men?

—No.

"I want to introduce you," I tell him when I'm dressed, "To my husband's first wife. She likes to think of herself as a patron of the arts."

Does he know what you're doing?

—No. Yes. In the moment... no. But he figures it out. Quickly.

When you stop returning his texts and calls?

—Something like that.

I disapprove. Cowardly.

—I don't deny that.

And then it's done. I text Annie. "He's into older women. She's into artists." Annie takes care of the rest: excited to be helping Zia, thrilled for my involvement. I don't know what happens, what information or misinformation goes back and forth between them until Zia calls me, demands that I drive her to his studio.

You agree?
—I don't know how to say no.
That's funny.

I think, maybe, she suspects something? Wants to make me uncomfortable? "I'm terrible with addresses," she says. I do text him to let him know I'm bringing "the person I mentioned, my husband's ex" to see his art. I insist he wait in front of the house—the idea of walking her into the studio, for whatever reason, seems repugnant.

And when we pull up, there he is. Posing on the lawn, leaning against the silver birch.

I hear Zia catch her breath. Follow her gaze.

Yes, beautiful like a god. More beautiful than his pictures.

Not beautiful enough.

Still.

Not without his uses. I don't get out of the car. Pull away from the curb before Zia reaches him.

Still feel a little like a pimp or a procuress.

Wonder how on earth Annie thinks this is fun, like playing Cupid.

Realize that passing off a former lover to Zia is probably not what she had in mind.

But it's what I've done.

It seems sort of… appropriate. Karmic. Balanced.

No, it's not.

It's totally fucked.

Totally fucked. Totally hot. Hands around your ankles. Yeeess…

EMASCULATION

BRIAN'S MOTHER SAYS to me once, oh-so-sweetly, that I am so driven and ambitious—in other words, *good* at my job—in order to emasculate Brian. That emasculating her son is my prime motivation in pursuing my career.

To which I reply that she has done such a good job emasculating both of her sons, there is nothing left for me to do.

Brian's mother and I do not get along, but I don't have to endure her for long. The day I say *that* is the last time I see her. She dies, alone in her apartment in Toronto, a few months later. Brian and Julian fly to the funeral together, but without their wives. I plead Alexandra's age as an excuse to not attend. Annie doesn't go either. I don't know what Annie's excuse is—nor what her precise issues with our mother-in-law are. Perhaps she too has been accused of emasculating, overshadowing her husband.

Zia wants to go, to pay her "respects." But only if Brian pays for the ticket. I play the villain. Say, no fucking way.

Are you so driven and ambitious in order to emasculate your law professor husband?
—What do you think?
Honestly, I think it might have been a contributing factor. At some point.

—Seriously. You really think so?

You're contrary. And if I tell you it was to escape the trauma and taint of your childhood, you will claw at me again and—fucking don't. But I can tell this is all a preamble to giving the elusive Julian, aka Brian's brother, centre stage. It's time for him to step into the limelight. He's been texting you, "Have you talked to Annie." He's about to up the ante.

—How the hell do you know that?

I understand story. So. What does he do?

He texts, again.

What you need to understand: until that fall, until Annie's heartbreak, crisis, breakdown, whatever you want to call it, he never texts me, calls me. Talks to me, looks at me. He exists, in my world, as an extension of Annie and Brian… a barely visible extension of Annie, an unimportant extension of Brian.

Unobtrusive, unimportant.

Invisible.

He's been reaching out, steadily, for the past few weeks.

And you've been ignoring him. Steadily. Despite your concern for Annie.

—Yes.

This time, it's not an inquiry. It's an invitation. Date. Time: "Can I meet you for lunch? Today? 11:30, at the Trib? I need to talk about Annie. It's critical."

I can say no. It's short-notice and I am busy.

He is virtually a stranger.

Sasha's voice rings in my ears. "I'm worried about Annie. Will you?"

I said I would. And I'm worried about Annie too. Red eyes. How many weeks of crying now?

Fuck.

I text, "Yes."

We sit opposite each other, awkward, unconnected. He wants to be there as little as I do. He is hunched over, disappearing into his chair, into himself. I find myself unconsciously mirroring his position. I hate that. I straighten my shoulders, raise my head. Thrust my eyes at him. He lifts up his head—meets my gaze for a split-second—averts it. But it's enough. The pain in his eyes makes me want to vomit.

I get up. I need to leave. I'm going to go to the washroom, and then not come back…

"Elizabeth," he says. It might be the first time he's ever said my name. "Please."

I sit down.

"I don't know how much you know," he says. "Maybe nothing."

"Probably nothing," I say.

"Do you know Annie wants to leave me," he says, doesn't ask. Voice wooden-yet-awful.

I nod.

"Do you know it's because she thinks she's had an affair." Again, a statement, not a question. His phrasing… so curious.

"She thinks she's had an affair." Yes. Curious.

He's not looking at me, so he doesn't see my grimace and the shrug of my shoulders. But he will hear:

"Well, she calls it an affair," I say.

His eyes jump up from the table, to my face.

"So you know," he says.

206

I nod as the waiter materializes at my elbow. We both look at him, not exactly with loathing—OK, with loathing. He melts into the background.

"I know," I say.

"And you would agree with me…" he struggles. "You agree with me… that it's not real. That it's stupid… I mean… She never actually…"

His face burns. And so does mine. I do not want to talk about this with him. At all.

I say nothing.

"She thinks… she thinks… she says that it doesn't matter," he says finally. "That it doesn't matter that they never even met: that it was all text. She says the intent was there. That she would have—that she would have done it if she could have. If he would have." His eyes bore into me, and I flinch and I want to run away. "It was awful," he says after a pause. "When she told me. About how… how it affected her. When he wouldn't… It was awful."

"Julian," I say, and his name sounds strange on my lips. "Julian, I am so not the right person to be getting any kind of marital advice from."

He disappears into his chair again. His eyes close.

"I know," he says. "I know you and Brian have a totally fucked up thing." It's not judgement, it's a statement of fact, and I accept it. "But you see…" he says. Such long silence. "I love her so much," he says. "I love her so much."

"This is something you ought to tell her, not me," I say.

"I have," he says. "I have… I have tried." I hear Annie's voice in my head:

"I've been alone in that marriage, in that house, for so long!"

I look at this barely present, barely alive man and I don't know what the fuck he wants from me. So.

"What the fuck do you want from me?" I ask.

He flinches. Raises his head up—but closes his eyes.

"I did something horrible," he says. "Something really horrible."

Great. So Brian's brother was already fucking around.
—No. It's much worse.

It comes out in fits and spurts, in a mechanical, detached voice. First, it's a confession of his—malfunction, he calls it. "Depression?" I ask. He shrugs. "Whatever. Maybe it's just a fucked up personality." He repeats what Annie's said to me—acknowledges his effective absence from her life, in any real way, for years. "I have no excuses," he says, and I'm not sure if he's thinking of his mother, but I am, because I am married to her other son. We all develop different coping techniques

"There was this fog," he says. "But you don't want to hear about that."

"I don't want to hear about any of it," I say. He nods. Keeps on talking anyway. And through the fog: Annie. So vibrant, so alive—as he talks about her, he seems to get bigger and brighter, and I suddenly am so envious…

Envious? This feeling, it keeps on surfacing, does it not? Envious, yes. Explain.
—Envious. Stupid, no? I would never talk that way of Brian. He would never talk that way of me…

"Trying to pull me back, but getting tired, and emptier, and fuck, I was broken—I am broken—but I was not blind," he says. "But I had no idea what to do. No idea at all. I would have killed myself to remove myself from her life, to make it easier, if it wasn't for… I know her. I love her. It would have crushed her, even if she didn't love me anymore."

I don't know what's worse. How he's drawing out the story, or how you're drawing out the story he's drawing out.
—It's difficult.
It's boring. What the fuck did he do?

"It was on her computer one day," he says. "She didn't shut it down, close it, whatever. And there is was. A dating site profile. And it was so—it was so her. And it was so beautiful. Passionate, fascinating—so worthy of everything wonderful. That I couldn't give her, because I was so fucking…

"I couldn't let her go. I didn't know how to bring her back."

"So you created your own profile," I finish. "Jesus-fucking-Christ. It was all you?"

He nods. "It was wonderful," he says. "It was really wonderful. I could see right away—she was different. So happy. Floating." He keeps on talking, but I stop listening. I think of Annie—floating, I saw that too. So in love-lust. Entranced, enthralled.

And then, broken, destroyed on my bathroom floor.

"You fucking bastard," I say. Get up. "You selfish, stupid, fucking bastard."

"Elizabeth…"

"Fuck off," I say. I am so angry. "How could you? How could you?"

I leave.

Now this is interesting. I can't wait until you explain your motivation.
—I won't.

209

Really? Even more interesting.

The universe is mad. Nothing makes sense. I don't want to go back to the office. I don't want to go back home. I can't go fuck Stefan anymore, and I will not drink. I would run if I weren't wearing fucking heels. I think about taking them off and running barefoot, and I would, except it's December and it's cold...

"Is everything all right?" the waiter.

I grasp the lapels of his cheap black suit jacket.

"No," I choke out. Does he know me? Do I know him? I come here often enough...

You fuck the waiter?
—What the fuck is wrong with you?

He takes me into the cloak room. Puts me in a chair, and wraps me in my coat.

"Should I call you a cab?" he asks.

At least tell me you thought about fucking the waiter.
—Fine. Yes. I definitely thought that this particular crisis would be solved by having a stranger's cock shoved down my throat.
Just not that particular stranger's?
—SLAP.
Well, that is interesting too... You realize you're going to pay for that with immense pain in a while? But for now... why are you so upset?
—I don't know. I didn't know then. I still don't really know...

He brings me a glass of water. I don't cry or talk. I just... suffer, I suppose. For me? For Annie? I haven't a clue.

When I go home, I barely manage to stay conscious for Alexandra. Go to bed exhausted. Don't sleep all night: aware of Brian beside me.

Aware of just how much I don't love him.

RITUAL

I AGREE TO meet Annie after work because I feel… fuck, I don't know. Her husband is a prize idiot. Her suffering, in light of what he's told me, is doubly ridiculous. Doubly justified. Doubly awful. I feel pity, compassion, and shame.

The least I can do is meet her for five minutes.

Do you know—the woman you were at the beginning of the story—she would have found an excuse not to?
—I suppose.
Do you understand, now, why?
—I don't know.
Shall I tell you?
—No. I'm telling the story. Omissions, lies, and all.

She orders coffee, I order tea, and we sit down, awkward. The last time we saw each other, I had to peel her off a 20-year-old slut. And she wanted to know if I drink.

And I made her cry.

Of course, our current encounter is awful, embarrassing.

"Here," Annie thrusts a package at me. "Merry Christmas."

I unravel the gold string slowly. Frowning, not grateful. We never exchange gifts at Christmas, not the adults in the family. Brian's mother was a Grinch unrepentant, and her sons keep up her tradition.

"Why did you…" I start to say as I take off all the red wrapping paper.

They tumble into my lap.

Walnuts. Whole, shining walnuts.

Speechless.

I finger one. Then another.

"I know you can't take them home," Annie says. The words spill out of her in a rush. And I know she's anticipating… a refusal. An interruption. Words from me that will cause her pain.

I grit my teeth and say nothing.

"Here." She hands me a nut cracker.

I don't say, "How did you know?"

I don't say, "Thank you!"

I crack a nut. Hand it to her. Then another, for myself.

I don't get it.
—I'm getting there.

The thing about walnuts… the bowl of walnuts on the dining room table marks the beginning of Christmas for me the way the Advent calendar marks the beginning of the season for most people. It's one of the few—only—traditions and rituals that existed in my fucked up family home, and the only one I take with me when I run. It doesn't matter where I live: in a shared dorm, in a cruddy stinking prone-to-flooding basement suite, in a hotel—if Christmas is coming, a bowl of walnuts appears on the table, dresser—once, tank of the toilet, because there is no other furniture…

Sometimes, finding the nuts poses an almost insurmountable challenge—like the year I spent Christmas in Johannesburg. *Almost* insurmountable. Fuck an American soldier enthusiastically enough and it's amazing what he can find and liberate for you from the base…

Brian is allergic to nuts.

"Which nuts?" I ask when he tells me. All of them, it turns out. Peanuts, *and* tree nuts. For good measure, coconuts.

"How seriously?" I ask. He reaches into his pant pocket and shows me an Epi-pen.

"Oh," I say. I don't realize then, that I'm giving up… Vietnamese food. Thai food. The glorious comfort of peanut butter, banana, and honey sandwiches. When I do realize, in our early years together, it doesn't matter so much.

Love conquers all and all that shit.

Until our first Christmas, when I put out my bowl of walnuts and come home to find them gone. Replaced with mandarin oranges.

We have our first—biggest—nastiest fight. Nothing ever comes close.

He accuses me of being selfish, thoughtless, and trying to kill him. I accuse him of lacking the base social and communication skills required to be called a human being.

You reconcile by fucking.
—Yes. And yet not solving anything, not learning anything.

After that, I mark the beginning of the season by putting out a bowl of walnuts on the desk in my office. Travelling with walnuts when work takes me out of town in December.

I wasn't going to ask why you put a bowl of walnuts on the television when you came in.
—I wasn't going to tell you.
Merry Christmas, lover-mine.

I guess Annie sees them there? At the office. She comes by every once in a while, to drop something off, for Sasha, for Alexandra. I don't know that Brian ever sees my office. His relationship with my career is uneasy.

Because you're so driven and ambitious in order to emasculate him.
—And to support his ex-wife in the style to which she has become accustomed, don't forget.

Between the penultimate walnut and the last, I manage to look Annie in the eyes.

"Are you better?" I ask. She still looks thin, but not thinner. There's eyeliner around her eyes and mascara, which tells me she's got to be crying less.

"It comes and goes," she says after a long pause. "It comes and goes."

She looks at her hands, and then at the nut shells. Pushes them around.

"Can I tell you something?" she asks. "I know you don't want to know. But can I…"

I nod.

"I think I'm almost enjoying the suffering," she says. "Not as much as I did… the other. But the intensity of the pain… it's better than what I felt before. Which was nothing. And Julian…" she pauses. I see her searching for something that it's OK to say about her husband. Fail.

If I were her girlfriend, I would probably say, "He loves you so much."

Instead, I just nod, as if she had told me the thing she needed to say. She nods back. "I can only think in awful clichés at the moment," she says, apologetic. "Life goes on. Left foot, right foot, breathe. You know?"

And then, she bursts into tears. "And it was all over nothing. Jesus, Elizabeth. Imagine what a pathetic wreck I would be if something really bad happened to me." And she laughs. I try to laugh with her.

We crack the last nut. Walk out of the coffee shop together. She hugs me goodbye and I let her.

And as I watch her walk away—again, I am envious.

Again. Yes. I told you. Of the suffering?
—Of her capacity for suffering? How she is embracing it, in a way? I feel… I envy her the angst, the madness of the love affair. Just as I envied Julian his suffering. His love for her…
Because you do not love your husband. Or your lovers.
—I did not.
"Did not"? I like that.
—Assumptions. It is not all about you.
Everything is about me, I've told you that, too. But keep on talking about the envy. You envied Julian's love for her. You envy her suffering…
—Yes. It seems exquisite—as she names it, I can see the pleasure she gets from her pain. Because it underscores the intensity of the pleasure that was… however fucked up, unreal, unworthy it really was. And maybe it wasn't unworthy if this is the result? If this is how she mourns it, how she feels?
Her suffering invites you to explore your own.
—I've told you not to psychoanalyze me.
You invite it. Shall I make you suffer in a more pleasurable way?

—Please.

Beg a little more ardently. And bring me to my first climax. You've had several, and an epiphany. Now it's my turn...

MUSE

WALNUTS ASIDE, I hate Christmas. So does Brian, and so making Christmas joyful for Sasha fell to me even before Alexandra was born. I do all the things—OK, actually I outsource most of them. Someone puts lights on the house. Professional tree trimmers do the tree, although Alexandra and her nannies add their homemade decorations.

This year, Sasha hangs mistletoe in the hallway and in the arch between the dining room and living room.

"What?" she says when I raise my eyebrows. "I'm hoping to have one of my girls over."

I smile. I almost say, "And you need an excuse to kiss her?" but that seems like teasing banter that's outside our usual interaction and I think she might misinterpret it and so I say nothing. But I smile, again.

I order turkey, side dishes, desserts from the Westin. I endure an afternoon of baking cookies with Alexandra and the nanny. Brian walks into the kitchen to see me covered with flour. He laughs. Kisses me, his daughter. For a brief moment, we look like a happy family.

I buy Alexandra earrings. Gloves. A scarf knitted by someone else's grandmother. Slippers. And an iTunes card.

A bag of wooden clothes pins for Sasha.

Funny.

—I'll include a cheque.
Of course.

And, in return for the walnuts, I buy Annie a new vibrator and a gift card to A Little More Interesting.

So fucking out of character. Describe the vibrator.
—Use your fucking imagination. There really isn't that much variety in sex toy form or function.

I'm at the sex shop looking at vibrators when Stefan texts me. And I go rigid. I don't want to hear that it went well with Zia. I don't want to hear that it didn't go well with Zia. I don't want to hear anything. I'm done with him and I want him out of my life.

Heartless bitch.
—He prefers another word.
Wise man.

All the text says is: "I finished. Do you want to see it?"
At first I don't understand. And then, I realize—the painting. The birch, the wig, the silly ballet shoes. The intoxication of being a prop, being posed.
He finished.
I am inexplicably proud. Glad. He finished. It won't be one of the unfinished canvases littering his studio.
I don't want to see it. No, not true. I would like to see it. Or maybe not. Actually, no. I don't want to see it. I think, in my imagination at this moment, it is better than it can possibly be in reality, in the execution of this derivative, mediocre painter who...
Fuck, what's wrong with me?

"I would love to see it," I type. "But I do not want to come to see it. Do you understand?"

"You don't trust me to not be able to keep my cock in my pants at the sight of you?" the text jeers at me, more cruelly than he ever would in real life.

I deserve it. And so, I am kind.

"Perhaps I don't trust myself," I type, although it isn't true.

And, I add, "I'm so glad you finished it." I pause. I want this conversation to be over. I don't want him to say anything else. I add:

"xx."

The painting is waiting at my house when I get home. It's huge. Bigger than me: I'd forgotten how large the canvas was. Wrapped in brown paper, fragile stickers all over it.

"A Christmas gift from a grateful client?" Brian asks. I shake my head. "Will you not unwrap it?" he asks. Fingers a label.

"Where's Alexandra?" I ask.

"Sasha took her to the mall. Christmas shopping. Will you not unwrap it?" he repeats. And tugs at a corner.

"Go ahead," I say. Turn my back.

"Holy-Mother-of-God," Brian says. I'm still not looking. "Elizabeth. Jesus. Look!"

I look.

Is it terrible?

—It's incredible. It's the best thing he's ever painted. Maybe the best thing he will ever paint. The sort of thing any painter—*any* painter—would aspire to. Never achieve. It is, truly, a work of art. I lose my breath.

The birch in Stefan's painting is so vivid, I can almost smell its bark—and it's bitter, sweet, fresh, and decaying all at once. That magical light he was blathering on about—it makes me believe in god. What he's done with the blonde wig, the golden ballet shoes, the yellow leaves—the light on my naked skin… I'm captivated by it all.

In that moment, I want him again.

Perverse.

—Typical.

Yes, I suppose. Was it my work that first made you want me?

—No. Don't you remember?

No. You'll have to remind me. But not now. What happens? Do you take Stefan back from Zia?

—He's not mine to take back.

By that logic, he was not yours to give in the first place.

—Logic. Fuck.

Let's. On the bed. Legs spread. I like the torturous-regretfully-totally-fucked-up-passed-off lover subplot, a lot.

I need to tell him. Oblivious of Brian, I take out my phone. What do I say?

"Thank you. It is… incredible."

"Is that… is that you?" Brian asks.

I nod. He's standing beside me. Then behind me. Tugs at my jacket.

"Take off your clothes." Voice hoarse. "Copy that pose."

"Alexandra…"

"They just left. They won't be back for hours."

The phone pings as I slide out of my suit jacket.

"I call it, 'The Cunt.'"

What do I say to that?

"It's the best thing I've seen you paint," I type back. Brian pulls off my pants.

"Who is this artist?" he breathes into my ear. "Someone you met at that gallery opening we went to? Back in May?"

Stefan: "It's the best thing I will ever paint."

"Yes," I answer. Brian's hands, rough, on my breasts. Shirt and bra off.

"Pose."

I pose.

Cunt.

Does he fuck you?

—No. He masturbates. To the visual of me holding the pose, in front of the painting.

Yesss.

CHRISTMAS DAY

I CAN'T REMEMBER at which point, exactly, Annie invites herself, Julian, and *Zia,* fucking Zia! over for Christmas Day dinner. There must have been discussion and negotiation, clearly—I don't fucking remember. Was it back in October, November?

You were too self-involved. I'm not the only one with narcissistic tendencies.
—Shall we say, I was distracted? Too busy watching Annie unravel... and getting Zia a lover? And I suspect I said yes to Zia's presence at least in part because I was feeling a twinge of guilt over not raising her living allowance.

Annie reminds me of this via text Christmas morning. "Merry Christmas! And you are so awesome for having Zia over!" She knows better than to add "I love you," but I can see she thought about it.

Narci-ssis-tic ten-den-cies.
—Ama-teur psycho-ana-lyst.
Every patient needs a therapist. Continue.

Annie and Julian are the first to arrive. Annie looks good, eyes less hollow, cheeks fuller. She's hefting a huge bag of presents. "For the girls," she says. Hugs Brian. Calls up the stairs to Sasha and Alexandra. Reaches for me and I meet her half-way, but it's awkward—I'm glad the bag gets in the way. She dances out of the hallway into the living room to distribute the presents under the tree. "I'll check to make sure the Westin delivery's all OK!" she shouts over her shoulder. Of course, why trust the caterers to do their job properly? I chase the thought away, unworthy, unnecessary.

Julian shuffles after her, slowly. I intercept him.

"Have you told her?" I ask him. He shakes his head. Flushes a spotted red.

"But I've told her…" he says, "I've told her the idea of her with other people? That it turns me on. That if it's something she would like to do… she could… she doesn't have to leave to… she could, it would…" his voice trails off. And I stare at him with a complete lack of comprehension. Is this love? Or is it utter idiocy?

It's his kink.
—But it's not. He's doing it for her.
Then maybe it is love. I don't know very much about these things. But I see it perturbs you. That amuses me.
—What?
Your overwhelming latent conventionality.

Sasha and Alexandra are coming down the stairs when the doorbell rings again.

"I'll get it," Alexandra cries out and races down the staircase, into the hall, to the door. I take a moment to glory in her joy; I take a moment to hope this will not be the worst Christmas ever. I'm practicing non-resentment; I'm practicing not resenting having Annie in my kitchen. Zia in my life…

"It's Zia," Alexandra announces. I decide to be a hostess and welcome the ex-wife into her former house on Christmas Day. I walk into the entry way. And there is Zia, taking off a fur coat.

And behind her…

Stefan.

Oh-my-fucking-god.

My fault, of course. Always, my fault.

What the hell was I thinking?

You just told me. Remember? You weren't interested in being someone else's sugar momma. Or fucking a derivative, talentless artist who wouldn't amount to anything. And you were tired of Zia whining. And Annie told you to play Cupid.

Also, you were evil.

—Well. Fuck. Yes. All that. I clearly thought nothing of consequences.

I don't know, at this point, if Zia knows? Oh, fuck, what is there to know? I don't know if she knows that… Brian continues to fuck this grad student, that one (how can she not? She certainly insinuates enough).

I don't know if she knows I know that Brian fucks around and I don't care (do I? I don't, I fucking don't). And I don't know if she knows that I… retaliate. Certainly, my first two lovers were retaliation.

Now, they are just habit.

SLAP. That's for reducing me to a habit.

—In this moment, at this time, you are allowed to think you are something different. An exception.

But am I just a habit?

—A lovely habit.

SLAP. Continue the story. It is engrossing, so I will try to forgive you…

I'm so pleased that the Stefan hand-off goes… well, smoothly. That she asks no questions. That he asks no questions.

I'm certainly not expecting the end result to be Stefan, at my house, on Christmas.

Crazy bitch, stupid cunt.

"Why are you here?" I hiss at him as Zia saunters into the living room and leaves the two of us alone in the hallway.

"Why the fuck did you set me up with your husband's ex-wife?" he counters. Hands into his hair, theatrical, but he's genuinely upset. Of course. Christ. What a situation.

"I didn't," I lie. "I introduced you to a potential client. Patron."

We both know I'm lying.

"You wanted nothing to do with me the moment you found out I was divorcing," he says. And we both know it's true. "You couldn't wait to hand me off."

"You let yourself be handed off," I say. He turns red. Eyes into the floor.

"Does she know?" I ask him. He shakes his head. Bites his lip.

"Maybe?" he says, finally. "I don't know."

"Stefan? Are you coming?" Zia's voice, from the living room.

"I'm so sorry," he says as he turns. "Do you believe… please, believe. She didn't say… where we were going. I didn't ask, because… it's my first Christmas alone, without the kids, and I…" He says nothing, but I know—anything not to be alone.

"I had no idea—you'd be here," he adds. "Please. Believe me."

"Of course," I say. Who'd walk into this shit show willingly? I follow him into the living room, where there's punch (non-alcoholic) and mimosas (prepared with club soda, not champagne) and a couple of bottles of wine, and also a bottle of Scotch, for Brian and Julian. When I next look at him, Stefan is downing a Scotch—not tasting it at all, it's all about downing it, and preparing for the second one—and his discomfort relaxes me.

"Brian?" Zia says. "Have you met Stefan? My date?"

Who brings a date to a Christmas Day family dinner? Rebellious teens. A courting "I'm going to marry that girl someday" student.

And Zia.

Zia.

Rattled, unhappy.

Why is it that she's still mourning Brian? This man I don't love, don't want, but have?

If I could, would I give him back?

"He's gorgeous!" Annie whispers in my ear. "Zia's boy toy? I love him! Look at him! I'm so happy for her!"

Annie.

Deluded, always focused on other people's problems so she doesn't have to face up to her own.

Brian's brother: he and I briefly exchange glances. His eyes say, life doesn't matter. What do mine say?

I don't want to know. I close them. When I open them, there is a pile of shredded wrapping paper on the floor. Alexandra is dancing in the middle of the room in her rainbow-ribbon dress, and Annie, looking at her, is aglow with joy.

"I let her open it early," she says, stealing a shy look at me. "Is that OK?"

I nod.

It's going to be fine. Everything's going to be fine.

And it almost is. Until we move into the dining room. And Zia sits opposite Stefan's painting.

Of you. Naked. In front of the birch in his garden. Tell me. Does she recognize the tree—the body—or the artist's style?

—She's never seen me naked or near-naked. And she would not think of that as my face. And I don't know that she would recognize the tree... or his style. That painting is so different from everything he's ever done, and, Christ, a tree's just a tree... But she's just spent a lot of time in Stefan's studio. So she's seen the sketches for this one... And, actually... seen *that* fucking painting.

Oops.

The scene unfolds like something from a horrible movie—and again, my life is a cliché.

She looks. Looks again. "Stefan!" she exclaims. "You didn't tell me you sold 'The Birch!' How wonderful! Did Brian get it for you for Christmas, Elizabeth?" The three of us react, in turn, like deer caught in long-beams on a highway. Stefan stares at her. At the painting. At me. Gulps.

I can't believe Brian put it up. I stare at him. He stares at me. Then Stefan.

Yes. Love it. Fucking get on top of me and finish me here. Now.

—*Now?*

Now. To the tension of "before it all comes tumbling down." Talk while you ride me, but fucking make me come.

228

"I understood it was a gift from the artist," he says. Turns his eyes back to me. "I put it up for you this morning, when you were out with Alexandra," he says, carefully, almost apologetically, "because I knew how much you loved it..."

"Stefan's the artist," Zia announces as if she is making a huge revelation. I catch my breath and I feel Stefan relax a little. Brian tilts his head and looks at Zia. Stefan. Me. The painting. Starts to connect the dots and I hope to god he connects them silently.

"How thrilling to meet you," Brian says calmly. "And who's ready for turkey?"

"Me!" Alexandra and I both shout, she in hunger and excitement, me in gratitude.

And we eat.

As we chew, Zia keeps on looking up at the painting. Stefan's eyes drill into his plate. Brian puts a hand on my knee.

"What the fuck did you do, Liz?" he whispers into my ear as he passes me the cranberry sauce. I stare at him in despair.

What the fuck did you do, Liz? Do it again, faster...

"I don't know," I whisper back. "Jesus Christ, I don't know." And we both look at Zia. Looking at the painting. Waiting for the explosion.

Coming, almost...
—Hurry...

"Stefan thinks it's his best work," she offers at one point. Bragging, preening. He's hers. "But I think he's capable of more."

Aaaah…

"I'm sure he is," Annie says enthusiastically. "It's a beautiful painting. Tell me," she asks something incomprehensible about paint mixing and scraping, and Stefan answers, shyly, hesitantly, then with increasing pleasure. They are animated and involved, and Zia frowns, left out, angry. I go rigid. And so does Sasha. Our eyes meet and I realize we're both looking for a distraction. Who to get her to focus on, talk to?

…mmmmm…

"Zia," I say, desperate. "Did you know that Julian…" and I pause, because I have no idea what to say about Julian, how to connect Julian to Zia—how the fuck does Annie do this all the time with people, the only thing that I know about Julian is that he's his own wife's fake lover, and what can I do with that information, nothing—and I look at Julian to plead with him, to say, please, for fuck's sake, help, do *something…*

…and I see him, staring at Annie—animated Annie, talking Annie, deep in conversation with Stefan—and he is entranced.

He is in love.

Fuck, yes. Did I miss anything important?
—Maybe.
Don't backtrack. I'll figure it out…

She is, in this moment, happy. And her happiness causes him joy.

Meanwhile, the frowns on Zia's face get deeper.

"Mom," Sasha's voice. "Mom?"

Zia's eyes, pulled from Stefan and Annie reluctantly, go to her daughter.

"How long have you known Stefan?" she asks.

Three weeks. I know.

"Three weeks," Zia answers.

"Not very long, is it," Sasha. Ironic. I'm shocked. Then appalled. She's not going to... She is. "Not very long. It's so odd, to want to bring someone you've only dated for three weeks to a family Christmas dinner."

"Sasha!" Brian's voice. I sink into my chair. Want to crawl under the table. Alexandra's beside me, and I squeeze her little hand. Focus on her. Does she have enough turkey, salad?

"I'm just saying..."

"Respect your mother!"

"How dare you!"

"What's going on?" Annie.

Silence.

"I'm going to go to the living room and get more wine," I get up. "Can I refresh anyone's drink? Stefan? Another Scotch?"

"Please," he says, smiles. Turns back to Annie.

"I think you've had enough," Zia says.

Ouch. Shadows of the soon-to-be-ex-wife.
—And not lost on him. That's the moment, by the way, that she loses him—the moment that he decides that he's been kept by a bitch before, and he's not going to do it again. But he just smiles at her—and looks at me—and says, again, "Please."

When I come back, Stefan, Annie, and Julian are standing in front of the painting. Julian's arm is around Annie's waist.

231

I meet his gaze as I hand Stefan his Scotch. His eyes say, "Maybe life is worth living." Mine fill with tears.

Brian and Sasha are clearing the table. Zia is staring, in naked hatred, at her alcohol-free punch, and at the trio in front of the painting.

Alexandra is still eating.

"I've decided to leave no room for dessert!" she announces blissfully.

"Awesome," I say. Follow Sasha and Brian into the kitchen, where Sasha bursts into tears.

"She's going to ruin Christmas," she says. "She's going to ruin Alexandra's Christmas."

Shall I tell you this is the moment in which you realize how much you love your stepdaughter?
—You. Shall. Not.

"She's not," I command. "She's not. We're not. It will be fine."

When we go back into the dining room, Zia's draped around Stefan. In front of the painting. Asking questions he does not want to answer.

That's when Julian produces the camera.

"A family photo, before we sit down to dessert?" he suggests.

And we dutifully assemble.

And the explosion? Does it come after?
—Miraculously, no. We eat dessert. Hold it all together long enough for Alexandra to have "the best Christmas ever."

The explosion comes the next day.

CAST-OFFS

BRIAN WAKES ME up early in the morning, tongue on my earlobe, hand on my ass, then fingers caressing my cunt lips. "What have you done, Elizabeth?" he whispers, lazily, into my ear as he nibbles it.

He's turned on.
—You think? That's utterly fucked.
He's turned on. As was I.

We have quiet, languid sex, slow and unexciting but thoroughly pleasant...

Talk about damning with faint praise!
—No, it's one of my loveliest memories of him!
Well, I hope that is not how you ever remember me. Fuck.

...and then I laze around in bed while he showers and feeds Alexandra turkey left-overs for breakfast. I'm still in bed when the two of them leave to do a Boxing Day sled on St. Andrew's Hill. And I'm still in bed when the doorbell rings.

On the way downstairs, I check my phone. A text. From Stefan. 4 a.m.

"She knows. And she's fucking livid."

And she's at the door?

She's at the door. She flies through the door as I open it, screaming, and runs past me and through the hallway and into the dining room where Stefan's painting hangs. And the only thought I have is that if she harms my painting I will kill the fucking bitch.

She stands in the middle of the dining room and stares at me and screams. And there are no words, just screaming, but I realize—fuck, I realize I deserve it. I was stupid, thoughtless.

A little evil.
—You said that already.

And so I take it. And as she finally makes words, "And how dare you think I would take your fucking cast-offs!" and grabs the vase full of dead bamboo that's a gift from Annie and hurls it at the floor, I'm grateful that she's breaking only that.

And not your painting.
—Yes.

She screams. And screams. I breathe. Stand in front of the painting to protect it…

Stupid idea. Posing with the trigger in the background.
—Well, those are not the terms in which I'm thinking.

…and stupidly, unintentionally, slip into escapist fantasy. I'm in Stefan's studio and I'm back in the chair, that first day. He's sketching. Soon, he will stop and come to me and fingers will slip into my cunt and…

"Are you even listening to me?" Zia screams and snaps me out of it. And... I lose it. I lose my fantasy, my detachment. My sense of guilt and my feeling that I deserve this.

"No," I say. I teeter just on this side of a scream...

That line you won't cross...
—I will not be fucking Zia.
But you will finally tell fucking Zia... what?

"I am not listening to you," I say. I look at her. My reality. My consequence. Fucking hell. Fifteen years. "I stopped listening to you years ago," I say. Pause. "What's the point? You only say one thing. The tape never changes."

She's screaming about Stefan today—but she's not, not really. She's screaming about Brian. Her wrecked marriage. Her wrecked life.

How it's all my fault...

I have a flashback, as vivid as a video clip—me, Brian, and Zia in his study, a decade ago, five years after the fucking divorce. Alexandra at my breast, Zia screaming and me, for the first time, the only time, screaming back: "I should be paying attention to the baby. Or sleeping. Not listening to yet another venomous attack by your bitter cunt of an ex-wife who still hasn't moved on, and who blames me for everything. You know what? I blame me too. I shouldn't have fucked Brian. God knows I didn't want to marry Brian..."

And Zia, if I recall right, doing nothing with the weapon you handed her...
—That's right.
Brian not alluding to it either, I remember. Hard to say which of the three of you has the worst coping strategies. I

think, overall, you're in the lead. But you've got worthwhile competitors.

—It's not a competition.

Says the second wife who hands off a lover to the ex-wife she loathes. It sort of is.

"The tape never changes," I repeat.

I look at Zia and I'm… angry. Sorry. And exhausted, so fucking exhausted. Shall I say it again?

No.

No more.

Enough.

I'm done.

Instead: "Leave. Get the fuck out of this house. And. Don't. Come. Back."

Zia stares at me, her mouth first an O-shape, because I interrupt her mid-scream, then collapsing into a slashed line. Tears swim in her eyes and they're about to burst—fuck. I do not want to see her cry—I know she doesn't want me to see her cry. She turns around and walks—not storms, not runs, *walks*—out of the dining room. I hear the front door open, close—not slam.

I manage to pull out a chair; collapse into it. Beyond exhausted. Ashamed.

Free? Fuck.

I wish.

You didn't scream. You weren't Zia. But you've crossed some other line, did you not, my lover.

—Yes. I did. And I'm about to cross yet another one…

236

VIOLATION

ON THE DINING room table is Zia's purse, where she threw it during her tantrum. It is red, gaudy, expensive. Paid for with money taken from my daughter, the beast inside me whispers. I try to suppress the thought then let it come. Allow myself, for a moment, to feel anger that, 15 years later, Brian is still supporting this woman.

I am supporting this woman.

The purse is tipped over and open, and as I lean over to move it—I want it out of my sight—anger surges in me again and I throw it. It slams against the wall, hits the edge of Stefan's painting.

The painting tilts. The purse's contents spill.

I don't move from the chair.

I stare at the crooked painting. The wall. The purse. Its exposed contents.

I *hate*.

There are few things, I think, more violating than going through a woman's purse. I don't know if men have an equivalent; I think not. I lose it even when Alexandra picks my purse up. And I have no secrets in it.

Well, perhaps the pouch of condoms and lube.
—That's not really a secret. Just an inconvenient truth.

I hate.

And so, I kneel down. Look.

I don't pretend I'm doing this to clean up, put away.

I am going to violate Zia.

And I will tell her. Or leave proof, so that she knows.

I hate.

There are the usual things. A compact. An outrageously expensive brand of mascara, the secret to Zia's whore lashes. Black eyeliner. A hairbrush.

Random, messy receipts.

A wallet, thick and bulging. So many credit cards. I methodically pull each one out. No cash. Not even coins.

No pictures of Sasha in the wallet. But then, in the age of smart phones, that means nothing.

A container labeled "Prozac." Figures. And—clearly not working, I let myself think.

A crumpled up program from Theatre Calgary for *A Christmas Carol.*

No profound secrets.

I gather up everything—don't bother to put the credit cards back in the wallet—and toss it all back into the purse.

I wait for shame to come. But it doesn't.

I'm still so angry. So full of hate.

And... disappointed.

From where came that?

I realize I'm disappointed because, in this act of deliberate violation, I was hoping, some part of me was hoping... to find a clue. To understand. Why, for the past 15 years, she's been playing that same role, the same scene. Not moving on. Not writing Brian off as a youthful mistake—as I should have...

...oh fuck did I just think that?

You did.

—I did. And, appalled, I sit with the thought. And let the next one come...

Is that the big secret, the reason for all the drama, the madness? That she still loves Brian with a passion and ferocity of which I'm not capable?

Not capable of loving Brian *with passion and ferocity or not capable at all?*
—What do you think?
I am wondering. I would never accuse you—here, like this, I think it's time I started tormenting your tits, those nipples are screaming for all the worst kinds of attention—of lacking passion and ferocity. But... at your most open, intimate, passionate, you talk of me as someone you love to fuck, not someone you love.
—You would run screaming if I said I love you.
You don't know that.
—Yes, I do.

I sit with that thought, let the question sit on me, heavy, unanswered. I wait, but remorse and shame do not come.

But self-preservation and a modicum of common sense return.

I dump out the purse contents again. Replace the credit cards in the wallet slots as best as I can remember. She may notice, of course, but she now has the option of pretending nothing happened.

Pretending I didn't look.

I put the purse in the hallway, by the door.

When Brian and Alexandra come home, I tell him, "If Zia calls about her purse, tell her it's by the door. Put it on the porch for her if she comes to pick it up."

"What?" Brian says.

"Or perhaps you'd better go drop it off," I say. "I told her not to come back here, ever."

And with that, I circle an arm around Alexandra's shoulders and leave the room.

I'm using my child as a shield to protect myself from further interaction with my husband.

That's when the shame comes, and it's all encompassing.

AGAIN WITH THE CONFESSION

I DON'T HEAR Brian tell me he's going to take Zia's purse back to her, and I don't hear him ask me what happened, and I don't hear him leave, and I don't hear him come back. I think about checking in with Stefan to make sure he's OK, but decide he can fucking well take care of himself. I watch bad Christmas movies with Alexandra, and fall asleep with her on the couch. I do hear Sasha tip-toe through the living room and I hear another voice, giggling. Her new lover. Then all is silent. When I wake up in the morning, Alexandra has another movie on.

"I stayed up all night!" she claims, but she looks much too happy and well-rested for that to be the truth. I don't challenge her. Get us bowls of cereal.

We're on our second morning movie when we hear Sasha let her girlfriend out. Alexandra giggles when she hears the "I love you's" and "kisses." Makes kissy noises at Sasha when Sasha comes in. The three of us are sitting on the couch, on the fourth movie of the day, when Brian comes in.

Looks at us.

Bursts into tears. And leaves the room.

"Are you going to go after him?" Sasha asks.

"Do you think I should?" I ask her stupidly and she looks at me with a mixture of disbelief and contempt and so I get up. And slowly, reluctantly go up the stairs.

What are you afraid of?
—This…

Brian is sitting on our bed, face in his hands, weeping. I don't want to sit beside him, and I don't want to stand, so I pull out the laundry basket from its corner towards the bed, and prop myself up on it. I'm not sure what to say.

Jesus, for a lawyer, you're bad at conversation.
—I know exactly what to ask to get the answer I want. Asking when you fucking well know you don't want to hear the answer is another matter altogether.

It doesn't matter, though, because just like Annie, Brian does not need me to prompt. He just starts to talk. The words come, and almost as soon as they come, I stop listening.

I don't hear what Brian is saying, I don't want to hear what he is saying. He's there in the room with me, I suppose, yes, he's there, sitting on the bed. Leaning forward. No longer crying, but eyes teary. Or are my eyes teary? I cannot tell. There is a wall between us. Maybe not a wall—a sheet of glass. Sound-proofed glass, and his breath, expelled with each word I don't hear, is clouding it over, and soon, I cannot see him at all.

I suppose that's all right.

I think well-trained Catholic priests don't actually see the sinners nor hear their confessions. Right?

It's a self-defence thing.

A self-protection act. A boundary.

The confession is good for the penitent. Not so much for the confessor.

Certainly, Brian's confession, 15 years ago, that he was fucking me, did nothing for Zia. Or rather, it plunged her into... well, whatever place she has been in ever since... for the past decade and a half.

Is it a confession if it occurs after discovery?
—It is if there is intent of atonement. And he sure as fuck would have taken atonement over divorce and me as his second wife.

This confession to me that he has fucked Zia is offering him relief, clearly, but it is doing nothing for me.

Or rather...

It's doing too much.

I try to make myself be rational. To think. How many women over the years? How much permission, however tacitly given?

What did I say?

"Be careful, and don't leave evidence around."

And also, "Never in our bed."
—That, too. My one caveat.

Because... I would not be Zia. I would not be the mad, stalking jealous wife.

And my Alexandra. A tiny clump of splitting cells at that moment of first discovery... And she would not be born into anger and recrimination.

And now what?

I raise my eyes from my feet and try to look at Brian. But there he is, still behind that clouded glass wall. I can't hear him. I don't want to see him.

I don't know what to do.

I know this act of marital infidelity—or marital return, depending on how you view it—is different than the grad student of the moment.

And I experience a surge of anger at Brian for being so fucking cliché. And dull. And low initiative. Could he not look, hunt farther away from home? Grad student after grad student. Our cleaner. Nannies, I bet. And now, the ex-wife. Fucking go farther afield!

I know I don't love my husband, the father of my child.

But... I've grown attached to him, and this I know too. He is, perhaps, an ineffectual father to Sasha... but how could he be otherwise, given the dynamic Zia has created?

But he is a good father to Alexandra. They sing together. Read books, he rarely misses a night of read-alouds with her, and I miss so many. All the chauffeuring he does, to choir, to horse camps.

Without a murmur.

The nannies we've had over the years have been little more than housekeepers. Alexandra had, always, two involved parents who loved her.

Who love her.

He more hands on than I, often, because, career.

And distraction lovers.
—Fuck. You. My lovers never took away from my daughter.
I apologize. Withdraw. Fully. Inappropriate.

Our family, at its most important level, worked. For Alexandra.

"Can you ever forgive me?" Brian says, and that breaks through the wall.

And I know I can forgive—anything.

But should I?

No, wrong question. I can forgive anything. And I do. I can even understand. I can see it. Zia, mad in her pain and anger. Stefan. Cast-offs. Elizabeth, that fucking bitch, do

244

you know what she... How dare you... And then, ejected from the house that used to be her house—and again I think, oh holy fuck, why did we not sell this place and move, why did we not have her take it—because, stone's throw from the university, because Brian's tenure, because it was the rational thing to do, because it had been his house first, because, like me, she had never liked it. All rational reasons. All wrong.

I can imagine Zia's pain, anger, state.

And I know Brian's... weakness? Softness? Whatever—soft heart. Perhaps it's a strength.

And I realize, suddenly, that when he goes to her condo, bearing that violated purse—that may be the first time they are alone together since she left.

Most of the interactions over the last 15 years have witnesses: lawyers. Mediators. A frightened Destiny, an angry Sasha.

Annie.

Me. And almost always, almost all of the interactions: at our house. In a parents' counsel about Sasha.

Always, always, witnesses.

And today—or rather, last night. Alone. Finally. Her pain, tears. A scream of "Unjust! Unfair!" from her lips. His guilt.

Her pain. His guilt, sharper, bigger.

Her rage. His response.

He draws her into his arms and she sobs. He caresses her hair, her back. He whispers... oh, what? What else. "I'm so sorry."

She sobs more.

"I'm so sorry," he whispers again, and he really is. "Zia, I'm so sorry for everything."

And then, what? An accidental brush of lips against skin, fingertips against bare flesh. Once, there had been immense passion between those two people. There is nothing but passion in Zia. I have first-hand experience of Brian's passion.

And so. They come together. And explode. And fuck.

I think I can probably handle the fucking. I could put that behind me. Here's the thing that's killing me, that's been killing me since I went into that purse searching for god knows what and finding nothing—that's been on the edge of my consciousness for months, maybe years, maybe from the beginning. My throat constricts.

"Does she still love you?" I ask.

I make the words loud, clear. I'm not sure if the cloudy glass between us is a one-way or two-way phenomenon. Can he hear me? "Does she still love you?" I repeat.

And the glass falls, breaks, shatters, tiny pieces fall all around us, and I see Brian's shocked eyes.

"What?"

"Does she still love you?" I say for the third time.

His face goes white. Then red.

Does he understand why I'm asking? Does he understand that if she loves him—I can't keep him, not even for Alexandra? Because... because I don't. Because, he could be gone tomorrow and I would mourn him for Alexandra's sake, but otherwise... fuck.

I don't love him and I have not loved him for 15 years. Does she?

Does she?
—Surely, she does.
Does he love her?
—Does it matter? Would not one person loving be enough?
Common sense and all the poets and pop artists are against you, lover. But you have fucking tears in your eyes. Come here.

—Don't.

Come here. If you don't cry because you need to, you'll cry because I'll slap you and you'll think that's OK.

—You have not unlocked me.

Perhaps not. But you've shown me a hell of a lot of clues to where the key is. And I see the fucking keyhole. Come. Here.

"Does she still love you?" I say again.

"You don't," he names the truth. I nod.

And I realize that it's that truth that must determine what I do. Not Zia's feelings, nor Brian's.

And I cry.

Cry.

—It hurts.

I know. Do it.

I cry.

FETTERED, FREE

BRIAN AND I fall asleep, fully clothed, on top of the sheets. We don't actually talk about anything more—we sit there, hold each other, and exhaust each other with our presence. I later find out Sasha peeks in—"I was a little worried that maybe you murdered him," she confesses, and she's only half-joking, and we both only half-laugh—and after ensuring we're both breathing, puts Alexandra to bed.

When I wake up in the morning, I am… ecstatic.

I kiss Brian on the forehead. Pull away from him as he, instinctively, still asleep, tries to pull me into an embrace. When his eyes open and he looks at me, he is not ecstatic. But he is tranquil, mostly.

"Did we decide anything?" he asks me.

"We're getting a divorce," I say. "And we're going to be terrific co-parents."

He's silent for a while, eyes open, eyes closed, hands under the covers.

He's totally playing with his cock.
—Don't all men, most of the time?
Touché. Continue.

"Elizabeth? You're not doing this… you're not doing this so that Zia and I…" he falters. "Because I don't know if…"

I nod. Then shake my head.

"No," I tell him. "This is all about me." Then leave him to shower. Dress. Check on the girls.

Your daughters.
—Our daughters. My daughters.

I pass the rest of Christmas vacation in a different kind of haze. I take Alexandra to the movies and lunch. Chauffeur Sasha a bit, and suggest she ought to get a driver's license. Ask if we're going to meet her new girl. "Eventually," she says after a pause. "I sort of seem to rush everything. I'm just going to wait and see this time. If she's going to stick around, I'll introduce you." I nod. She gives me an odd look. I flush. I know it's because it's the first time I've asked, anything. I don't want her to make a big deal out of it.

I check in with Stefan, just to say, "Everything's OK here. You doing OK?" Him: "The scratches are cosmetic and will heal. I'll forgive you in time, but only because of the painting. And for fuck's sake, never, ever do that to anyone else. Um... she didn't damage the painting?" Me: "I promise. Painting's fine. Happy New Year."

I am...

Free?
—Not the word I was searching for, no. How can I be free? I am a mother, stepmother. And I have made a child with this man—this is my lesson from Brian and Zia's marriage, from the last 15 years—I am fettered to him, effectively, forever.
Interesting. Because, you know, this is the modern woman's fantasy. To be free—in order to be owned by someone else.

—Not mine.

Then why are you here?

—You know why.

Say it.

—Feel it.

Mmmm, yes...

Brian wants to put off telling the girls. I overrule him. "Now," I say. "I need them to know. Now." I let him have a few days, but I want it done. And, ultimately, so does he. The man who was terrified of being divorced and alone at 40 is OK with it in his mid-fifties.

Do you know why?

—Yes. Do you?

I do. But I'm dying to hear your misinterpretation.

—Maybe he's learned that being alone—not that he will ever be alone if he doesn't choose it, not the way he is—is not nearly as bad as being married to me.

Self-loathing does not become you, Elizabeth.

—I am, finally, free of self-loathing. Mostly.

Telling Alexandra is, simultaneously, hard and anti-climactic.

She is singing and drawing, and she barely raises her head from her easel.

"It's OK, Mom."

Not her job to solace me and I tell her so. And I start to tell her that Daddy and I are both really happy about this decision, but she interrupts me.

"You and Daddy aren't really married, anyway. You're more like roommates."

Pain shoots through me. So it was all for nothing? Me, faking it, enduring it, living the lie, all that time? All for nothing? She knew, all along...

"You're good roommates, though," she adds, quickly. "Are you going to keep on living together?" she asks, her left hand drawing meticulous lines.

"We'll probably get two houses," I say. We haven't discussed it. But fuck, I want to get out of this house that was never mine.

"OK," she says. "Not too far from each other, OK? Walking distance would be best."

She keeps on drawing. I don't know if she's OK or repressing.

You're going to put her in therapy, aren't you?
—Fuck, yeah. God knows she won't be able to talk to me.
Where's Brian during this encounter, by the way?
—Talking with Sasha.

I say more things. She murmurs things back. I don't know if I broke her or if I saved her.

We all get broken.
—If you speak one more cliché at me...
You'll what?
—I'll stop telling the story.
Then I will be silent. Or try to, anyway.

Brian comes into the room as the front door slams.

"I told Sasha," he says. "Alexandra, my love, you good?" Alexandra drops her pencil, gets up, and runs into his arms. I watch them embrace. Brian beckons me over. I join them, and I'm relieved to see tears on Alexandra's face. I kiss some of them and Brian kisses some of the others.

"Sasha's angry," he says. I nod. That, I expected.

I don't ask him if he's told Zia. I don't care.

Not true.

—Mmmm. True enough.

Now. For the most important part of the story.

—What's that?

Annie. Do you tell Annie? And does she get to keep you?

—I'll tell you. But first, about Sasha.

I know what happens with Sasha.

—How can you? I don't know myself until it happens.

Oh, Elizabeth. Fine. I'll indulge you. Pretend you don't know. Tell me what you don't know, my deluded, lying, beautiful lover.

ABSOLUTION

I LOSE MY clarity and happiness when that front door slams behind Sasha. Even as I watch Brian hold Alexandra, I want to text Stefan, with a totally inappropriate, "Wanna fuck?" Call an ex-lover. Find a new one.

Even the waiter from the Tribune?
—Anyone.

I am terrified. I've fucked up my daughter's life, and my stepdaughter—I did it to her, again, again, and she will never forgive me. In my head, I can hear Sasha, yelling at Brian: "So you divorced my mother, ruined her life, mine, for something temporary?"

And what is my responsibility towards an ex-stepdaughter? Is there such a thing? That morning, for the first time, ever, I thought of "our daughters, my daughters." But I have undone that. There is no such thing.

Alexandra's apparent peace throughout the day soothes me, but after she goes to bed and Brian goes out—to see Zia? To see someone else?—I go into the kitchen and lay my head down on the kitchen table, and wish I wasn't afraid to drink.

"Jesus, Elizabeth, is this how you cope with stress?" Sasha's voice. In the doorway. I lift up my eyes, my head, my body.

"I don't so much cope with stress as I ignore it," I say. I get up. "Do you... um, do you want... coffee?"

I glance at the clock. It's almost midnight. If we drink coffee now, we won't sleep.

"Yeah," Sasha says. I go for the beans and grinder. She sits at the table. Waits while I whirr. While the water boils.

I put a cup of black coffee in front of her. "No sugar, right?" I ask, because I'm not sure.

"No sugar," she says. Takes a sip. "Holy fuck, it's fucking tar."

"Yeah," I agree. "I like it chewy." I inhale the smell.

I am terrified of this child. Her future. My responsibility.

"I wanted to ask you something," she says. I nod. Brace myself for... recriminations. Hate. Guilt. Shame. All the things. Instead: "I know you guys haven't talked about any logistics. Or anything." Pause. "But... I just wanted to know... can I live with you?"

"What?" I don't hear her right, I misunderstand her.

"Can I live with you and Alexandra?" she says. "I mean, not all the time. Or forever. I mean, fuck, I'm 20. I want to... you know. I want to have my own place and all that, and soon. But until then. And when I don't. Can I live with you?"

Time stops. Everything is still, perfectly still. I can hear my heart, her heart. Our breath.

"Ah... of course. Yes," I say. "Always."

She nods.

"I thought so," she says. "But I thought I should ask." She gets up, in one long, quick fluid motion. "This coffee is like fucking motor oil, Elizabeth. If you want to sleep at all this week, you shouldn't drink it. Next time, let me grind the beans, OK?"

And she leaves.

Her coffee cup is empty.

She drank the tar.
—She drank the tar.

So I drink mine. Sleep like the dead until noon the following morning.

THRESHOLD

SO. ANNIE.
—ANNIE.

I don't know how one tells a sister-in-law that one is leaving her husband's brother, and I appreciate, finally, why Annie's attempt to tell me...

"You are very important to me."
"Family is very important to me."
"I don't want to lose you."

...was so fucking awkward. So I don't tell her, and when she shows up on my doorstep mid-day on New Year's Eve, livid, I just let things get more awkward as I open the door and wait for her to save my ass by starting the conversation the way she always does. But she says nothing, just walks past me, into the house, and into the kitchen.

I follow her and watch her. She's boiling water. Grinding coffee. In the kitchen that's not my kitchen. Is it Brian's? Brian and Zia's? Who the fuck knows?

Just not mine. I think of myself again as an interlude—a 15-year interlude, just that, nothing more.

Interloper, you said before.

—Interloper. Interlude. Same thing.

Self-pity becomes you as little as self-loathing.

—Fucking indulge me. I'm in not-my-kitchen with not-my-sister-in-law and I'm scared.

Of what?

"Fucking! Bitch!" Annie shouts suddenly and I jump.

"Did you hurt yourself?" I ask.

"Were you not going to say anything, ever?" she demands. Turns towards me, on me. Angry.

"Is it over then?" she asks. "I mean, you and me?"

I know what she's asking and I feel bad. Awful. Because there was never a "you and me"—no Annie and Elizabeth. It was always her trying—and me blocking, evading, resenting. Can the last few weeks when I was more present make up for 15 years of detachment?

"I'm so sorry," I apologize. For the past. For being the person I was. Still am.

So, she hears, "Yes." She turns her body and head away from me, faces the stove, kettle, grinder. Busies her hands.

Maybe there are tears swimming in her eyes.

Maybe there are things she wants to say to me.

She preps the Bodum. Reaches for mugs. She is at home here—as she was before me. As she will be after me.

"Tea for me, please," I say mechanically, because I never drink coffee with Annie.

"Fuck you," Annie's voice is shrill. "I know. I know you drink coffee. And you'd just never drink coffee with me. Today, you're having a fucking cup."

There are tears in her voice, and when she turns back to face me, in her eyes.

"Fuck. You." She repeats, looking at me. I've never heard her swear like this, and it's a marvel. "Fuck, fuck, fuck you! I tried so hard. I tried so hard to... anything. Be your friend.

To... love you... Because...." Her voice trails off. The silence that follows is oppressive.

"Because?" I ask. I'm not sure if I want to know. But I can't bear the silence.

"Because! We were family! We are family! And you..." the mugs finally come down on the table, the coffee mostly unspilled. She folds into a chair. "And you... so disconnected. Wanting nothing to do... with any of us."

I wonder who she includes in her universe of "us." Herself and Zia? Herself and Sasha? All three? Alexandra? Are Brian and Julian part of "us" too, or is it a universe composed only of women and their bonds?

This thought: does her eagerness, the need to build these bonds with women stem from Julian's effective absence, from her long-term marriage of one?

If Annie and I were friends, I would perhaps tell her why my ability to bond with women is so impaired.

But we're not.

I don't know how to... I don't even know how to tell her why I don't know how to love her.

I don't understand, still, why she needs to love me...

"The only reason I kept trying—you were such a cold-hearted, nasty bitch, such a cunt," Annie is now undammed, all the things she did not say to me for 15 years flowing out of her, "the only reason I kept on trying is because you were so good to Sasha." Her voice breaks. Tears come. "I tried so hard with her too," she says. "I love her so much. I love both your daughters so much. But they don't... Sasha... I was never what she needed. I could never tell what she really needed—could never give her what she needed. You could. You did."

Her head droops, and tears streak down her cheeks, into the coffee cup. I, rigid, finally sit down.

"I'm so sorry," I say, again. "I'm so sorry." I wish I could undam with her. Find words. Voice anger, resentment, shame. Regret. Instead, I reach for the coffee mug. Embrace it with both hands and let the heat pulse through me, warm me.

Your relationship with the black drug is almost erotic.
—To you, everything is erotic. I am coming as close now as I ever will to revealing the tragedy of my life. To her. To you. And you're getting hard again.
Tragedy is erotic. The things that make you laugh don't make you hard. Or wet, lover, as the case may be. Check yourself. You are telling me the tragedy of your life... and you're dripping.
—That would be because I'm straddling your face and you're licking me. And, fuck you.
That's getting old: you have, you will. We are getting to that again. But continue to be my good little story teller first. Now. Where were you?

Kitchen. Annie. Coffee. Shame. Pain. Anger. Resentment. Regret.
Annie: "You're so... fuck, for years, I wondered if maybe you were a cyborg. Or clinically... Fuck. I know... I know why Brian fell for you. I know why, for someone living with Zia, the way you were was so appealing. Fuck. I know what his mother did to him, and to Julian." A pause. A look at me. "What happened to you, Elizabeth? What the fuck did your mother do to you?"
And she steps onto the threshold of my tragedy and challenges me to open the door. It's a moment that... if I say and do... if I accept her challenge—her invitation—if I give her the truth of me...

You will hear it, learn it yourself. And you're not ready.
—I'm not ready...

I do realize that perhaps it is time to talk of this to someone, anyone. And I even think... yeah, I could talk about it with Annie. I can see us, sitting—not at this kitchen table, not in this fucking house, somewhere else, maybe one of the coffee shops we think we can't go back to, but we will, we will be without Zia, and we will be brave, and go back—I can see us, sitting, drinking coffee. And me talking. Telling her. Her listening.

Understanding, maybe. Or not. But listening.

But I can't go there. Not yet.

"Do you know that poem, by Philip Larkin?" I say instead. Close my eyes to recall it. "'They fuck you up, your mum and dad'..."

"I do," Annie says. "It tells you they were 'fucked up in their turn'... and to not have any kids yourself."

"Yeah. Well. Too late for that, for Brian and me, anyway," I say. "And yet... all that matters is that I don't fuck up Alexandra the same way I was.... And Sasha... I don't know..." I don't know how to say that for the last 15 years, I've worried I had irretrievably damaged Sasha—first, by my intrusion on her nuclear family, and then, worse, by being the catalyst for Zia saying and doing those terrible things that night. Never mind all the nights, times since...

Atonement. Trying to save her. At least protect her, a little.

"Are you going to walk away from her too?" Annie asks me. She is blunt and cruel and out of character, because she wants to hurt me.

I deserve it, and so I take it. And say nothing in my defence.

"I hate you," she says. "I hate you, I hate you, I hate you."

I listen. I hear Zia, 15 years ago. Sasha, ten years ago—six months ago. Myself, at six, at sixteen.

"I'm not particularly fond of myself either," I say. And I look at Annie. I am on the cusp.

You won't cross it.
—I won't. But that moment—and this moment, here, right now—is as close as it comes.
Lover...
—If you fucking make me cry again, I'm going to leave.
You're not. I won't. But just in case—your snotty nose into my shoulder, like that, and hide your not-crying eyes against my neck...

She sees it, and her anger and hate evaporate. "Oh, Elizabeth," she whispers. And she becomes—that thing she is that I've resented and ran from and feared. And she wraps her arms around me and pulls me into the embrace she demanded from me when her heart was breaking on my bathroom floor... and bursts into tears.

As do I.

She holds me as I hold Alexandra—as I think I can now hold Sasha. "You don't fucking get to leave me, Elizabeth," she says into my ear. "Got it?"

"Got it," I whisper back. Hoarse. Exhausted.

Loved.

Safe.

AN UNSATISFACTORY ENDING

AND THEN?

—THAT'S it. That's all.

…

That, my lover, was a thoroughly unsatisfactory ending. In so many ways. Fuck, look at me. Completely disenchanted

—You wanted a true story. That is how it ends. I was a thoroughly unsatisfactory wife. But I found out I was an OK mother. And all those times I thought I was fucking up as a stepmother—not all bad, in the end.

I imagine you and Brian are stellar co-parents.

—We are.

And Brian and Zia?

—Well. There were reasons it didn't work the first time around, and it turns out it wasn't all my fault after all. Although I'm not sure Zia will ever forgive me. Still. It makes her happy that I am no longer Brian's wife— so that's resolution and a victory of sorts for her, right?

How very generous of you. She did not hook back up with Stefan?

—No. Although we're both following his career with great interest, and occasionally bump into him—and each other—at gallery openings. But he hasn't painted anything as good as 'The Cunt'—I mean 'The Birch'—yet.

Nor will he, I am sure, without you as muse. Still. You were a catalyst.

—Perhaps.

And Annie? Do you ever see her?

—We're in a fucking book club together. Without, miracle of miracles, Zia.

And you've bought, and are reading, the book?

—I have, I am. And Annie being who she is, I'm not sure how I will avoid being the godmother of the child she and Julian are currently expecting.

I'm so happy for them. Genuinely. Take me to the christening as your date. That will be a satisfactory ending to the story for me. I want to see all of them.

—I might. If you're around then.

I might be. Don't you think?

—No. I picked you because you are guaranteed to not be there, in the end.

Cunt. I will surprise you.

—Maybe.

Maybe.
Is that how it begins?

Yes.

an INVITATION

Thank you for reading *Consequences (of defensive adultery)* by M. Jane Colette. If you enjoyed the book, please consider taking the time to leave a review of it on GoodReads or your favourite bookseller's website.

Reviews matter—they make a difference, and they help feed authors.

WANT TO CONNECT?

Twitter + Instagram @mjanecolette
facebook.com/mjanecolette2
goodreads.com/mjanecolette
TellMe@mjanecolette.com

Ask Jane to send you love letters:
M. JANE COLETTE'S LOVE LETTERS
at mjanecolette.com/LoveLetters
to be the first to find out what's new from M. Jane Colette's, and to get free books and lots of love.

mjanecolette.com

ABOUT THE AUTHOR

M. JANE COLETTE writes tragedy for people who like to laugh, comedy for the melancholy, and erotica for women and men who like their fantasies real. She believes rules and hearts were made to be broken; ditto the constraints of genres.

*

Tell Me (2015)—an erotic romance for people who like a little bit of angst with their hot sex

Consequences (of defensive adultery) (2017)—an erotic tragedy (!) with a happy ending

Cherry Pie Cure (2017)—the award-winning "LOL rom-com for the sexting and blogging generation"

Text Me, Cupid (2018)-- a (slightly dirty) love story for 21st century adults

Rough Draft Confessions: not a guide to writing and selling erotica and romance but full of inside insight anyway (2017)—a non-fiction collection of essays about writing dirty and more

mjanecolette.com

Made in the USA
Columbia, SC
06 September 2018